I0620316

The Backdoor to Bliss
A Companion Guide to *Triangulating Bliss*
& Navigating Your Own Bliss Triangle

Janelle Jalbert

Synchron8
Publishing

Synchron8 Publishing
www.synchron8publishing.com

ISBN: 978-1-942535-06-5 (ebook)
ISBN: 978-1-942535-07-2 (paperback)

Table of Contents

Foreword i

Introduction 1

Behind the Scenes of *Bliss* 5

    How *Bliss* Came to Be? 7

    Deleted Scenes 27

Reader Resources 63

    Synopsis 65

    Character Sketches 73

    Bliss Triangle / Disappearance Timeline 81

Team Bliss 103

The Bliss Challenge 105

Cheat Sheets for Following Your Own Bliss 107

    5 Tips for Identifying Your Bliss / Purpose in Life 109

    5 Ways You Can Follow Your Bliss…No Matter Your
    Current Circumstances 111

    5 Tips for Adding a Little Magic to Your Life 115

    Tips for Handling Loss, Change & Challenges 121

Extended Excerpt of *Triangulating Self* 125

    Teaser 125

    Excerpt 127

    The Mystique of Living Series 141

About the Author 143

Connect 147

Follow your bliss and the Universe will open doors for you
where there were only walls

~ Joseph Campbell

Foreword

Triangulating Bliss is special and close to my heart. Yes, every author believes that the tales they create are extraordinary. Writing a novel is truly like having a baby. The initial time of conception is one of joy and ecstasy, as the perfect story is acknowledged, even if only as a vision of the ideal and all the potential at comes with it. Then, the task of getting that perfection translated into the imperfect world of the written word begins. Writing is an art and a study in approximation in many ways. The nuances of words and their combination bring both success, when it works well, and reconciliation, when reality approaches that golden expression but can't quite nail it down concretely.

Then, the baby is born. In the case of writing, birth comes at the moment you finish the working draft, not the moment of publication. The youngest version of a full draft is when the real work begins. Like with children, the author-parent commences the task of shaping a piece, to the best of their abilities at the time, into a work that will be successful and make a mark on the world. It isn't easy. There are tough decisions to be made. The journey is filled with successes and learning opportunities. Yet, the goal of seeing that piece of you shine a light into the world fuels your drive through all of the highs and lows. So it is with writing…the same with parenting…as with living…and so too with finding your bliss.

080

This guide, for lack of a better word, encompasses all that *Triangulating Bliss* screamed out to be from the very start. Little did I know when the flash of a story premise hit me - much like how the Bliss Triangle appears to the characters in the novel - that I would go on such a monumental journey within the context of my "novel baby". As a life-long bibliophile, my favorite bookworm moments are when I am lost in a story or another world in truth. The hardest times are when the story that I have become so enmeshed in comes to an end. When those stories end, it is almost like I have to say goodbye to a part of my own life that I came to love and hold dear.

Of course, the real world is inescapable, at least on a permanent basis. Still, that little book-loving, story-believing girl in me will have a momentary fit. "I don't want it to end," she admits as the last page is turned or the last swipe of the e-reader is complete. "I want more," she says, even when the story in complete and satisfying. I've learned to pat that youngster on the head, agree that it was a great journey regardless of how long or short it was, and coax her to the next adventure. In this case though, I am blessed with *Triangulating Bliss*. I get to do something special for my young, inner bookworm and others who would like the story to continue just a bit longer. Even better, I get the chance to bring the fictional fantasy of the Bliss Triangle a little closer to the everyday world we encounter before us.

This companion guide pushes back the curtain and goes behind the scenes of *Triangulating Bliss.* Often, I have wanted to know more about the background of how a novel that impacts my life comes to rest in my hands and before my eyes. I've written plenty throughout my life, but no other piece has had such a force of its own both during its creation and also as an impact on life beyond the cover. *Triangulating Bliss* became a gift to me from above, however you choose to label what the "above" is for you. I am deeply grateful for the experience, regardless of the final outcome of the novel itself. In fact, I am more thankful than I can put into words. It is from this overwhelming sense of gratitude that I open up the backdoor to Bliss in order to share the gifts and spread a little more of the magic that is *Bliss*. I thank you for joining me on the journey.

Live, love, laugh, and most importantly, follow your bliss.

~ Janelle Jalbert

Introduction

Have you ever wanted to learn more about a treasured book? Did you ever wonder what the author was thinking or why characters did what they did? Is it possible for a work of fiction to help shape a better life in the real world? These are a few of the questions that *The Backdoor to Bliss,* as a companion guide to *Triangulating Bliss,* aims to address. This guide is broken into five, user-friendly sections: Behind the Scenes; Reader Resources / Book Club Notes; Triangulating Your Own Personal Bliss; Bliss Challenge; and an extended excerpt from *Triangulating Self.*

The title, *The Backdoor to Bliss,* comes from the opening line in chapter one where Greg opens the door to a life-changing place. It was purposely chosen as the backdoor rather than the front door because of real-life events in my life, as well as Greg's outlook on life at the time the story starts. Now, it has an additional significance because this guide serves to push back the curtain and take a behind-the-scenes look at *Triangulating Bliss.* Hence, the first section is dedicated to the story behind the novel and how it came to be. In addition to the background about the novel, details about the characters are expanded and deleted content is included with commentary about the decision to omit.

The second section is of a more traditional reader's guide. Discussion questions, insights, and elements to ponder about *Triangulating Bliss* are included.

Taking the story from fiction to reality, the third section dives deeper into the main theme of the story. Thoughts about how to identify, find, and follow your bliss are the focus. It sounds so neat and simple to just "follow your bliss" to your "happy place", but life is complicated and sometimes chaotic. What the heck is bliss, anyway? Can anyone and everyone follow their bliss? How does someone do so when the demands of daily life constantly tug at them? I'm not a psychologist, but finding true happiness, contentment, and bliss is really the purpose of living this crazy thing we call life. Like the characters in the novel, you are invited to go on own Bliss Quest. This section gives you a chance to explore what that all means.

As noted in the foreword to this guide, *Triangulating Bliss* took on a significance that went beyond the spinning of an interesting tale. It wasn't just about the journey to complete it for publication. It became something more as the characters took on lives of their own. It was Lois's tale that inspired the *Bliss Challenge*. Her purpose, after losing the love of her life, planted a seed for taking a fictional character and creating real-world good. Lois's call to "Follow Your Bliss" and her love of fairy godmothers make up the foundation for the *Bliss Challenge*. Learn how you have already stepped up to the *Bliss Challenge* as well as how you can continue to share the bliss.

The final section of *The Backdoor to Bliss* is a special bonus just for those who have decided to go behind the scenes of *Triangulating Bliss*. The novel ends with an excerpt from the follow up novel, *Triangulating Self,* which is Phil's story. However, *The Backdoor to Bliss* gives you an extended preview that is only available in this companion guide. Ultimately, the journey continues, but in true Phil fashion, you need to look back without going backwards, learn the lessons, and make peace to move ahead. You get the opportunity to enjoy more of what is to

2

come with a sneak peek to the tandem novel focused on Phil's side of the Bliss Triangle experience. You will get more of the details about who Phil was and how he came to be   the   man   behind   the   door.   Enjoy!

Behind the Scenes of *Bliss*

In this section, there is a brief description of how *Triangulating Bliss* came to exist. It goes from the first glimpse of the concept to the lead up to the book's release. There are insights into both the joys and challenges of getting a novel from concept to physical book. Following the discussion on how it came to be, a series of scenes from the initial draft of the novel are included. These scenes were either heavily edited or deleted from the final release. Consider it the "Director's Cut" (or Editor's Cut, in literary parlance) bonuses to *Triangulating Bliss.* There were various reasons for the changes during the editing process, but here you'll get to see what the original draft included.

How *Bliss* Came to Be?

The shortest possible answer relating to the exact moment of inspiration would be…it happened while walking out the door from a happy hour session with my "soul sister" Rebecca. Of course, it's not quite so simple. That's when lightning struck, but it took more than that to get me committed to writing. In fact, it took far more to get it from inspiration, through perspiration, along the path of refining, to completion. I wish I had done a journal entry marking that initial moment. Given how the story evolved, it would be interested to see what the moon was doing that evening in September of 2013 because, in fact, I did walk through a door into another world. I know it wasn't a full moon because I was in Charlotte a week or two later when a crazy full moon hit. It may have been a new moon, which again would make perfect sense given the Bliss Triangle. But, I digress. The story of Bliss most likely began in 2010.

In 2010, I was living a dream…something that would have been a true pipe dream a little over a year earlier. I began writing on the side from my job as an online professor. First, it was about education since I was also working on a doctorate in the field. Then, I got a seemingly random idea to pitch to an editor for a job covering motorsports, since I have a love of racing. He said yes. Months later, I was writing and doing photography at tracks around the country. It was a highly unlikely development given that I had spent the previous decade teaching language and literature in middle schools and high schools in Los Angeles. Still, I was there, in the pits, in the garage, and all over the country.

Six months after I did my first on-track assignment, I packed up my car, my computer, my camera, and all of the books that I needed to complete my comprehensive exam for my doctorate program. I drove east and landed in Charlotte for a month of living out of hotels, Starbucks shops, and my car. Not only was I traveling to tracks, I was teaching online courses and had 30 days to complete three academic research papers that would determine if I moved on to my dissertation. Oh yeah, and I began the journey east with the most hellacious hangover since college, thanks to an eventful send off with Rebecca...but that's a story for another time.

I covered events in Kansas, South Carolina, Delaware, Charlotte, and Texas during that period, without once getting on a plane. I amazed my comps professor with my papers too. But, the real game changer was signing a lease to an apartment in North Carolina. I returned after that month back East to cover the race at Sonoma, and then repeated the process. I packed up my car and drove to North Carolina where the keys to my apartment awaited.

It was an amazing year. The world seemed ever expanding. Everything seemed to click except for a few hiccups. The wind smelled sweeter. The colors were brighter. Everything was fresh and interesting, if not plain exciting. I was truly living the dream and then some. As a girl, I wanted to be a writer and when I was told to do something more "practical", I added teaching to the mix. I picked teaching because I figured it would let me be geographically mobile. I got bit by the travel bug at age eight with a cross country family trip and had already done a fair amount of international travel. Now, I was once again roaming the country seeing new places. I was writing for a national recognized outlet, and I had found a way to add my unlikely racing passion into the mix as well. After all, most sports reporters don't come from the ranks of the high school and college English classes, and they most definitely don't major in linguistics and education. Life was good. Then the bottom fell out.

I had feelings for a month or so that things were developing. It appeared on the periphery of my vision like distance dark storm clouds far out on the horizon. Things began happening that made everything that was bright and easy become heavy and burdensome. Then those dark clouds were overhead, literally and figuratively. The love of my life at the time, my 10 month old pup, died suddenly on the couch one stormy Monday evening. Yeah, it may sound melodramatic and even a bit odd given the catalyst was the death of a dog. I admit that, but it is far more simplified than the truth of the entire situation. The reality was that my life was rocked when my guardian angel in a fur suit left.

A year to the day after I picked up my apartment keys in North Carolina, I was pulling back into the driveway in California. For two years, I bounced along the road of life like the proverbial kicked can. While I was in Charlotte I had three bylines, two online teaching jobs, and a doctoral program that I was using to launch a business as a college admissions counselor. By the time I returned, I had stopped writing and had one teaching position. I was still charging ahead with my dissertation though my advisor threw up roadblocks faster than Caltrans and the university kept changing the rules.

Two years later, even that one teaching assignment was down from four classes for 50 weeks out of the year, to one at a time. I worked on starting up a marketing business, but it was fairly lackluster. My fortieth birthday was approaching, and I made peace with leaving my doctoral studies. It was a hard decision. Money had a lot to do with it, including student loans the equivalent of a mortgage. Really though, as much as I loved learning and education I had come to distain the system. That makes getting a doctorate in education pretty ridiculous.

Since I left Charlotte in 2011, I had made it a point to go "home" in the spring and fall for a visit. It was the pressure release value to handle all of the stuff in California that had originally fueled my relocation. As time passed, my visits started to get longer because being there allowed me to be myself again. I booked my spring trip to Charlotte to start aboard a red eye flight that left L.A. thirty minutes after my official birthday ended. It was supposed to be symbolic of the new leaf I'd turn over with forty. Thirty-seven had rocked. Thirty-eight and thirty-nine? Definitely not. This was to be the line in the sand.

Over the course of the next two months, it seemed like my declaration to the universe for the fresh start was working. People came into my life that surprised me. My business got a boost out of the blue. The frustration of beating my head against the doctoral wall was gone. I even had the chance to extend my single 10 day trip to Charlotte into two trips that covered most of that two month period. It wasn't an instant turnaround, but I did see some light at the end of the tunnel. When the teaching job that I held for the previous five years vanished without notice, I didn't see it as the catastrophe it would have been a few months earlier.

That fall, the familiar "off" feeling from 2010 began to color the edges of my world again. Normally, my fall visits to North Carolina are in October, but as September approached I began to hear a little voice. "If you're going, you have to go sooner or not at all." It wasn't a one-time thing either. I heeded the warning, and booked a trip for the last ten days in September.

It was a few days before that trip that I met Rebecca at Gus's in South Pasadena for a Wednesday Happy Hour / Chill Out. I hadn't been there before that day. I walked in through the backdoor and into the bar/lounge area. I sat down at the bar, ordered a Southern Sangria, and waited for Rebecca to arrive from work.

It has a history, that place. I felt it right away, and it wrapped itself around me as we passed the evening. We talked about my upcoming trip to North Carolina, which

Rebecca was unexplainably hesitant about. I figured her feeling was about the fact that it wasn't going according the usual schedule. We talked about how life was treating us and how we were both getting rundown. As we closed our tabs, we mused about how much we wish things in life were different.

As I held the door open for Rebecca to follow I mused, "Wouldn't it be great if you could walk out the door and walk right into your perfect reality?"

Rebecca acknowledged it with a shrug and a mumble.

"Seriously, that's a great story idea!" I got excited instantly. It was the first time in decades I thought about fiction writing. Thinking of my happy hour buzz and not wanting to forget inspiration, I added, "Remind me about this tomorrow. I'm serious. I don't want to forget."

Well, she did forget all about it. I didn't. The next morning the wheels were starting to turn in my head. I sent her a message: "You forgot but I didn't". Then, I let it all percolate. The bubbling became the piles of random notes that typically litter a writer's desk, coffee table, computer and whatever other surfaces where sticky notes, index cards, Word documents, and note pads can rest.

As I packed for my trip to Charlotte, that little voice kicked in again. "You've got to write this."

"I know." I mumbled back to the empty air around me.

I took my collection of notes in my carry-on. I vowed to get the bones of the story going during the trip. Still, the cross between going home and a vacation presented its own distractions.

The biggest detour came when I was at one of my favorite hangouts one night. A good friend of mine with whom I had reconnected with after years of silence was working, so I settled in for the night. I had one of the regulars chatting me up most of the night and was happy to see him go after far too many tall tales and my too-polite-to-tell-him-to-buzz-off persona being in control. After relaxing into some relative peace, another regular I knew from back while living in North Carolina walked up behind me and planted a kiss on my neck. That was the straw that broke my polite exterior. The annoyance grew as my friend just shrugged it off after admitting that he watched it all go down. I walked out for some air and saw a reddish full moon.

"I swear it's a redneck moon," I stated to my friend when he slid a fresh bear in front of me.

"It's North Carolina. They all are," the New York native retorted, and I couldn't help but laugh.

Restaurant workers from a neighboring business came in for a couple of rounds. By then I was on point, and they quickly realized that they were barking up the wrong tree with their moves. They cleared out leaving the bar area empty except for one couple in the far-back high top. I didn't notice the woman making her way to me.

"Hi. We saw you here dealing with everything tonight. We thought you'd might like to join us."

Here we go again. I thought. *I just want to chill.* I did the polite smile and shook my head. "I'm good. Thanks."

"Come on." She didn't want to give up and was trying to wave me that direction. "My husband's British."

Ugh. I wanted to grimace and laugh at the same time. *I know all about Brit males. No thanks. If she only knew.* "Thanks, but I'm happy here." Then the unspoken message came through loud and clear, and I almost spit my beer out. *Ah crap...they're fishing for a threesome. EEEW! Avoid eye contact and hope she gets the hint.*

She didn't. Instead she sat down. "I'm studying to be a palm reader. Mind if I read you?"

I have friends who are different degrees of psychic or spiritual or whatever you choose to call it. That doesn't put me off. I just wanted nothing to do with leaving my barstool. "Fine." I gave her my left hand, which I know is not the right one to read for a general read. That one's supposed to be about the past. It was part test and part convenience since she was to my left.

"Okay. Don't give me any clues. Try to stay as neutral as possible. I don't want you to influence me." She began examining my hand.

"Fine." I stated before taking another gulp. *I'll pretend you're not really here and focus on my beer as planned.* I thought.

She went on for a good fifteen to twenty minutes. I did an occasional grunt or nod or polite smile. I wasn't really paying attention. Like most guys who visited the restaurant, I was drinking beer and trying to follow the games on TV. Then she said something had the wheels in my head screeching to a halt.

"Mmmm," she shook her head. "You need to get your sh*t together."

My head swiveled to meet her gaze. Normally, I would say it was pretty brazen and witchy with a capital B, but I didn't. *She didn't just say that.* The words from one of my friends who does have a real gift resounded once again. That was two months ago, but he had said the exact same thing under equally random conditions. *"You need to get your sh*t together." Oh crap. Once is one thing...twice...Houston, we have a problem!* I ended the niceties as quickly as possible and sent her on her way with her hubby.

I had to regroup. I knew that but had been struggling with getting traction since I returned to California. The universe was speaking. I knew it, but I didn't have a comeback or a plan. That wasn't normal for me, and I was definitely alarmed.

It was the day after I returned from that trip that the little voice spoke to me again as I bounced around some ideas for the story. "You've got thirty days."

That's a bit melodramatic, don't you think? 30 days. Really?

"Thirty days. Yes. It will happen if you want it to."

13

"Thirty days? Why thirty days? Sounds like a Field of Dreams thing." I couldn't help but mutter. *Fine.* The itch to rise to a challenge overrode rational processing. *Let's see what happens.*

Silence…but the challenge was laid down.

I vowed to start the next day, but then decided not to put it off. I looked through my piles of notes and figured out that I wanted the main character to be a male, young but not stupid young. I wanted him to be addressing some sort of existential crisis. *Dropping out of law school when his family expected him to be a successful lawyer. Yeah. That's it.* I didn't see the parallel to my own life or doctoral journey at the time.

Okay…this guy is exploring mysterious disappearances. He's learning about the twists involved with them too. Somewhere down the line he'll experience it. Now, they go through the door. What do they see? The first thing that came to mind was Mikel's cartoon-like, *Gulliver's Travels* episode. It was still fantasy and colorful and hadn't taken the hard turn.

There's gonna be more than one…what next? Richard's disappearance came next. I saw him go through the door and immediately get slammed against the wall of a prison shower. *So much for walking into your perfect reality.* The story already began to take on a life of its own. I knew that the story was going to start with a newspaper article about Mikel's death, so I started with that as a prologue to what was to come. A couple of hours later, I smiled. I completed the opening scene.

o8o

Triangulating Bliss was its own unique journey. It often developed on its own along the way. In writing parlance, it was more of a "pantser" than a "planner" experience. I had the general idea when I began, but the twists and turns it took weren't anything I was prepared for at the start. I knew the basic set up of Greg's situation, the disappearances from a local bar/restaurant, and that Mikel's character would be introduced after having died - his family blaming Bliss for it all. Still, it wasn't until the second day of drafting that Bliss even got its name. Nope, this whole Bliss thing was not even on the radar in the beginning.

Bliss came to be while searching for a slightly ironic name for the restaurant in light of the main character being a man. It wasn't until "Bliss" came to mind that the true irony became clear in both the name of the place and the situation Greg found himself, without a clue of what came next in life. In fact, the name of the place, before Phil bought it, came first as an "of course" moment. To balance out the female nature of the name "Bliss", it was originally named "Smitty's" before "Our Place".

There's a funny story there. Once I finished the initial draft, I let Rebecca read the first three chapters. She was the one who brought it to my attention that there was actually a Smitty's in Pasadena that she swore the story was based on. I still have yet to get there, but I changed the name to "Stu's" to avoid any conflicts. Plus, it seemed that Stuart was to be an important factor down the line, if not right away.

In a situation reminiscent of Phil's comments to Sara about the universe sending more persistent signs and messages until you get it, I later found out that there is a little bar named "R Place" in Pasadena as well. Talk about crazy odds! I have never been to either place, though I hope to visit Smitty's in the future out of curiosity.

While getting *Triangulating Bliss* prepared for the world, many random people have brought the place up in conversation with me (without even knowing this story). I kept "Our Place" in the novel because it works so well with the storyline, and I don't think the businesses are the same. Smitty's officially became "Stu's". The decision was based on the original owner being named Stuart which came from the thought that the man was the original 'steward' of the special place that became Bliss. It was just one of those

15

gifts from the universe to see how things were linked even without any previous planning. I smile and like to think it's a sign of good things.

080

The 'voice' within that told me it had to be done in 30 days had seemed outlandish and unnecessary. Instead of questioning it, I took it as a challenge. It was the first of October, 2013, when I jumped in and dedicated myself to pounding on it daily, or for at least five days a week. I wasn't holding myself to the 30-day deadline officially, but I knew the story had to get out. The drafting of the story was honestly an enjoyable and often exhilarating journey that reignited my writing passions. I wrote anywhere from 1,500 to 3,000 words a day. It didn't develop in a linear manner either, which made each session more interesting. At the end of the day, I would chat with my dad about how it was going. I was happy that he was sharing in the evolution of *Triangulating Bliss*, and I was glad for the encouragement as well.

It wasn't until October 30th, that the little voice all made sense. I wasn't done. In fact, in the days prior to that life changing Wednesday, I'd stalled. I had come to love Lois, and after her story developed into the twist I hadn't seen coming, I just couldn't bear to let her go quite yet. As I was preparing to do what needed to be done, I found out that my dad took the day off of work to go to the doctor. That was unheard of for him, and I was alarmed by it all, especially after news had traveled my way that he was slurring words and had a problem with his balance. He rarely missed work because of health issues, and he most certainly never willfully went to the doctor.

That afternoon, dad returned with a diagnosis of a bladder infection that seemed to be ludicrous. The circumstances were so completely 'off' and wrong. The doctor had even mistakenly put my grandfather's name on the prescription instead of my dad's, and my grandpa had

16

been dead thirty years! I sat with my mom and argued that he needed to go to the emergency room and not just an urgent care because a bladder infection didn't explain his symptoms. There was a history of strokes in his family and the alarm bells went off in my mind.

Hours later, he walked back to his car for his obligatory book and told me that mom was taking him into the emergency room. Finally! I gave him a hug there in the driveway. It startled me how small he felt at that point. He was my dad - the larger than life hero since the day I was born - yet in that hug something had changed. It was the moment where the life I had known shifted to my new reality.

By the next morning (ironically, Halloween), the first rounds of tests were performed, and the diagnosis wasn't a bladder infection. It was a brain tumor. He was scheduled for surgery the following Sunday.

When the day came, I woke with a Florida Georgia Line, "Stay", playing in my head. My heart was heavy, but I didn't have a bad feeling about the procedure. I arrived at the hospital after he had been wheeled in and waited with my mom and sister as the Sunday race in Texas played out on the TV in the corner. Even my love of racing was muted at that point.

He made it through his surgery. My mom, sister, and I stayed in the waiting room until he came out of recovery. It was a long day that began before sunrise. My sister, Gina, was tired and her oxygen machine was getting depleted, so we did a quick visit before I planned to take her home to rest. As we walked into his room, a young nurse stopped the three of us. She looked between us and asked where she knew us from. My sister was the one that was habitually in and out of the CCI and ICU with her health problems for 13 years, and the staff knew our family pretty well. When the nurse placed us, she cried out, "No! But, you're such good people." That should have been a hint.

17

Gina and I remained with dad for about a half hour before deciding to go home. Mom was going to stay until dad got comfortable. We made it about ten feet from the door when the attending physician walked up to me asked if I knew what was going on. I've learned that saying yes is always the best way to be sure you are truly informed, especially in sensitive situations.

"Yes," I said as I tried to read the computer screen behind him.

Gina sat in her wheelchair to my right and remained silent. Two nurses circled around us.

"What happened?" The young doctor asked.

"What do you mean?" I countered.

"You know he has cancer, right?"

I knew the tumor meant cancer, but it was the first time the word was put out there in the open. "Yes."

The doctor looked at me like I had two heads. "What happened? I mean he had two tumors in his brain. It's in his lungs, kidneys, bladder, blood, bones…"

He kept listing places, but I had tuned him out by then. Time stopped. I looked at Gina, but I couldn't tell if she already knew or if it was as equally surprising to her. I shrugged. "He's stubborn," was all I could get out. Then irritation surfaced. It wasn't anger, yet. First, I was irritated with the doctor, continuing to list all of the places the cancer had spread in detail just seemed to be piling on unnecessarily.

I was in a fog as Gina and I went to the elevator and returned home. Life as I knew was officially ending. That night I begged God. "One more Thanksgiving." Then, I got greedy in a needy way, "One more Christmas."

The week after dad's surgery, I returned to *Bliss*. It wasn't easy. I was facing Lois's exit in the story combined with the knowledge that my dad's time was short.

Remarkably, he was released within 48 hours and returned home. He paced the driveway saying whispered prayers, and I would join the meandering to tell him where the story was going.

18

The day of Greg and Jen's first real date will always be with me. "They're going on a date," I started as we ambled down the driveway. "I have an idea of what they might do, but I'm not sure about the specifics yet."

"The characters have taken over, huh?" He asked quietly.

"Yep."

"That's what makes the best stories," he smiled. He was right. That's one of my favorite things about reading and writing. Sure enough, the couple gave me some pleasant and funny surprises.

o8o

The week before Thanksgiving, he was admitted back into the hospital. I felt a panic, not just because of his health. The first night he was in the hospital, I worked to complete the draft and pounded away at it.

I gave myself permission to claim one night for myself to celebrate, even while dealing with dad's health crisis. It was equally soul soothing and heart wrenching, but it was necessary. I printed a copy of the draft and drove up the coast to San Simeon to celebrate with the sea and some sparkling wine. The following day, I went straight to dad's room. I wanted to share the story with him...finally. It meant so much being that he was responsible for my love of the written word.

"I'm sorry. I can't," he explained as I offered the binder to him. "It's too hard to read."

"I'll read it to you," I offered.

He shook his head. "Sorry. I hurt too much."

My heart broke just a little more. The little girl in me was sad that the most important reader in my life couldn't read it.

Two days before Thanksgiving, dad returned home. We got one more Thanksgiving at home, though it was difficult for him to even sit at the table or try to eat anything. Dad worked to keep the holiday as normal as possible, but my heart broke with his discomfort.

I started editing the draft in the weeks between Thanksgiving and Christmas. It felt like my request for a Christmas was going to happen until the Friday beforehand. The doctor called while I was away from the house, and immediately dad was ordered to report back to the hospital.

We got that Christmas together, though it was in the hospital. After giving dad his Christmas presents, he told us to go home and enjoy Christmas Eve. When he called the house at 10:30, my heart ached because I knew the reality hit him. He was alone in the hospital during his favorite holiday. I packed my backpack and headed back to the hospital. Nothing was going to stop me from getting back in to be with him, and the way his face lit up when I appeared unannounced at his door was worth it all. We spent the night watching a John Wayne marathon before I dozed off for a while in the window seat.

o8o

I should have asked for one more of all of the holidays. At two in the afternoon on New Year's Day, the hospital called and said that we needed to return immediately, though mom had just left his side. My mom, sister, and I were with him when he made it official and let it ride. He passed before the sun rose the next day.

o8o

Life went sideways in more ways than I thought could be possible after that. Still, I did numerous edits on the novel until I won a book contract the following April. My attention shifted to drafting the *Wine for Beginners* book which had a 90-day deadline. "Luckily" (I put that in quotes intentionally…you'll see.), I was able to talk the editor of the wine book into pushing the deadline back from the end of July to August 15th.

On that Friday morning, I excitedly submitted the draft of the wine book and went to celebrate with my mom and sister. Instead of waiting until noon, I had pulled the trigger and then popped the cork before 9 a.m. I entered their house with a glass of bubbly after texting my "crew" that it was time to finally celebrate something in 2014. It was to be a happy weekend to blow off steam.

The party ended as soon as I got to the living room minutes later. My sister wasn't well, and mom said that they were likely headed to the emergency room.

An hour later, I helped lift my sister from the shower because she couldn't do it herself. When I lifted her into the car, that feeling returned. It felt like I saw death in her eyes. There was no blue, just black. Gina had already flat-lined by the time I got to the hospital. My little sister was pronounced dead at 8:00 that evening. Needless to say, *Bliss,* either as a novel or a pursuit, was the last thing on my mind.

080

The novel remained a file on my computer and a bunch of papers in a binder for nearly six months. When I opened it up again, the first thing I realized was the nature of Phil. Whether I meant to do it or not, Phil was my dad. Originally, I modeled the eyes on him and the rest on a friend of mine, but with the passing of some time, it became clear my dad was Phil. It was a mixture of happiness and sadness to come to that realization. I knew the book would be dedicated to him from the start, but I didn't get to share it with him in person. Still, he does live on through it.

The fact that *Triangulating Bliss* is fairly unique as a story premise proved to be a source of additional complications. For those who enjoy stories that add a little magic into daily life, the gatekeepers in publishing believe they just don't sell. The label of "Magical Realism" was quickly relegated to a secondary descriptor rather than a

21

primary genre. I hesitated to label it as women's fiction at first because the spotlight protagonist, Greg, is indeed a male. Plus, I saw it as a story that either gender can enjoy. I settled with the description of the novel as upmarket fiction with elements of "mystery, romance, a quest, and Magical Realism". That got a few more bites than leaving it as just Magical Realism.

Still, the finicky publishing powers that be remained persnickety. Those who are familiar with writing and publishing can understand the journey down into the rabbit hole for acceptance. My favorite episode came while talking with an agent at a writers' conference in San Diego. She read 20 pages of an early draft. That draft started with a prologue where Greg was in the coffee line and read about Mikel's death. It went through chapter one to the point where Greg walked into Bliss and waited to talk with Lois. (Since then the beginning evolved several times over to what it is now.) Granted, I knew the current attitude regarding the use of prologues, but I wanted the story to start with Greg walking through the backdoor of Bliss, and I still needed to establish that Greg was in the middle of dealing with a huge life change as he learned of Mikel's death. I wasn't surprised when the agent began with her distain for a prologue. I had heard that enough already. Instead of discussing the rest of the opening pages, she went into a tirade.

"People don't just disappear," she began.

"Yes, they do. That's part of the Magical Realism aspect."

She shook her head. "Well, you can't say they disappeared if they return," she countered.

"Why not? Any person who goes missing has 'disappeared' from their normal life for some period of time, right?" I shot back.

"Listen. I watch those shows on TV. You know CSI and Criminal Minds. People don't just vanish!" She was actually starting to levitate out of her chair with her outrage.

After handling a momentary shock and loss of words, I worked hard not to laugh out loud or grin. She just didn't get it and was bent on showing her superiority in the process. Referencing fictional TV stories as fact just cracked me up. I understood immediately that I'd never want to work with her anyway. Still, it taught me a lesson. You have to believe in your book baby, yourself, and understand that some people will react to your work in ways that have nothing to do with you, as a writer, or with the story itself.

I got into contact with an author, Julianne MacLean, who wrote an amazing book about near death experiences, *The Color of Heaven,* which she later turned into a series. We exchanged emails about the challenges of writing stories that don't quite fit the mold. She is far more established than I am at this point thanks to her romance writing, so she has an agent in place and experience with big publishers. She explained that she hit similar walls with her work. Her agent loved the book, but publishers didn't bite because of marketing concerns. Eventually, she went the self-publishing route after the manuscript collected dust for quite some time. I was glad to see the similarities in experiences, even if it was in line with the disappointing news that I expected.

After several rounds of submissions and revisions (I lost count after 17 edits and more than 50 submissions), I decided to bring it to life myself. The twists and turns continued.

My love of Lois's character spurred me to create the "Bliss Challenge" and raise money for Make-A-Wish (R) programs. It's also a way to honor my sister. She was disabled, but her life-threatening issues didn't develop until she was in her twenties. When the idea of raising money for Make-A-Wish (R) became reality, I had to change a few scenes in the story because I didn't feel it was appropriate to go with a more explicit love scene between Greg and Jen (not that it was a 50 Shades scenario or anything, but still.)

I also toned down some aspects of Richard's disappearance experience.

It's an interesting issue for a writer to take into account those aspects of their projects, especially since Richard's story was one of the strongest storylines being shouted at me throughout the drafting. Some may say that's selling out, but I see it as being reasonable because it doesn't impact the overall story arc.

The added time and distance also allowed for additional plot twists that didn't surface earlier. The relationship between Greg and Phil didn't emerge until three months before publication. That part of the storyline was a shocker, even for me. I consistently had problems with how Greg was perceived in earlier versions. I wanted him to be someone who was struggling with life issues without being seen as a "wuss" for taking into account his dad's influence and being unsure about his future. Originally, he was simply a guy in his late twenties who finally was taking charge of living life on his own terms. Still, I wasn't sure if it was working. The first change was to make him a returning soldier. That helped, but didn't quite fit. Then his would-be fiancée, Tara, emerged and the tangled web of the Ellison parents came to light. That's when Greg finally became rounded and grounded. It only took about two dozen edits and nearly two years of uncertainty. It proves that successful writing is often more about the revisions than the initial drafting.

Similarly, an emerging thread appeared during the numerous revision cycles that Phil's story, as the 'guardian' of the Bliss Triangle, was intriguing. I began to wonder why Phil was part of the whole thing to begin with. Plus, it is thought provoking to think about the nature of the great beyond and how reality as we know is perceived from the other side. The first thought was to create a sequel (since that seems to be all the rage). Once I stopped to think about it though, it seemed that Phil's story would be more of a prequel. As the outline took shape, even the notion of prequel didn't fit right, so I settled on the term "tandem".

It's probably more of a semantic issue, given my background in linguistics, but it feels right. Readers can view it however they wanted.

Hence, *Triangulating Self* started to take shape. When thinking about both the story and the nature of life, I began to understand that to truly find your bliss; you have to understand yourself and the concept of love, in all its forms. From there the workings of *The Mystique of Living* emerged. If you had told me two years ago that *Bliss* was anything more than a single novel, I would have laughed. Now it seems the Bliss Triangle has expanded its reach though.

o8o

Even the early stages of the launch process were filled with lessons in learning and evolution. I decided to create a webpage for the book with the domain name TriangulatingBliss.com. As the planning process continued, I stopped and asked myself "When was the last time I visited a book webpage for a fictional book?" Sure, non-fiction may lead me back to a website, and I may look up an author page from time to time. For a novel though? I couldn't think of a time.

Given that my personal life was marked with some intense challenges, and I was in the midst of what could be called a "middle life crisis" of sorts, I realized that what I wanted most in life was to be happy again. More specifically, I wanted to feel joy again. Part of my happiness comes from helping others, so the website became something bigger. Instead of being dedicated to the book, the site was dedicated to helping people pursue happiness and (in Lois's words) follow their bliss. That's how the story of *Bliss* is transforming into something bigger. Hopefully, it relates not only to an entertaining and thoughtful story, but it helps to make the world a better place, even if it's just through one reader at a time.

Deleted Scenes

The following scenes (chapters) were either completely deleted or heavily modified (edited) from the way they ultimately appear in the novel. These are the "first edition" drafts of selected areas. In some cases, added plot twists and developments aren't referenced as they occurred in later drafts. The selections are included as they were written, so there is the possibility of typos and minor grammatical issues present that were not corrected.

It can be interesting from both a writer and reader perspective to see how the final release evolves from what is initially drafted. Selections include: more backstory on both Henri and Sara, the more graphic depiction of Richard's experience, and a spicier, kitchen love scene between Greg and Jen.

Henri's Original Backstory

Greg knew it was Henri the second he came through the door of Bliss two days later. Jen stopped in midsentence having noticed the man as well. He was tall, toned, tan, with long sandy blond hair, but he dressed with a touch of Euro style. He wore a cream colored sweater, and his jeans were faded just right. Even his leather loafers had style. Jen thought, *I'd definitely enjoy a night out and a night cap with that one.* She didn't recognize the man, even after he introduced himself to Greg.

"Hi, I'm Henri Nevin," he said, after noting Greg was the only customer in the middle of the afternoon. "You've got to be Greg, right?"

"Yep. Please take a seat," Greg gestured Jen was oblivious to the fact she was staring. Greg cleared his throat to get Jen's attention. "I'll take a soda, if you don't mind." His tone was pointed, even a bit jealous.

"Oh, yes," Jen snapped back into her waitress role. "Can I get you anything?" She asked Henri.

"Yeah, I'll just take a glass of water for now," he paused. "You don't remember me, do you?"

Jen blinked. "Don't think so." The first thing she thought of when she saw this man walk in was the film from her theater trip during her disappearance.

Henri smiled. "I came in here quite for a while. You came from back East, didn't you?"

"Yes, North Carolina," Jen began to piece it together. "Oh, I remember now! You were taking care of your mom while she was fighting cancer," she paused. "You look great. A whole new look." She gestured at him. "It's been a while. How have you been?"

"I'm good. Spent the last several months working on getting my business ready to open," Henri smiled. Jen mirrored it, and Greg frowned.

"What was it you decided to do again?" Jen stepped closer to Henri. "A gym or something like that, right?"

"Wellness Center. It's part gym with different types of classes, a cafe, and a health center." He paused. "You know, you should come to our Grand Opening. It's this Saturday. Well, you...and Lois...of course."

"I'd like that. You'll have to give me your card," Jen smiled and went to get their drinks.

Greg was more annoyed at watching the two book a date than he cared to admit. "Thanks for coming, Henri. As you know, I'm researching a series of disappearances from here at Bliss. Lois mentioned that you had one."

"Yes. Last year. March 22nd to be exact. Can I borrow your pen for a sec?" Henri pulled out a business card. Greg obliged. To fill the void in conversation while Henri wrote his number down, he handed Greg a second card, "You're more than welcome too. The more the merrier."

Greg noticed that the Wellness Center was in Manhattan Beach. Greg nodded as acknowledgement but stayed silent.

Jen returned with the drinks and was more enthusiastic about the card and number than Greg liked. She complimented the card's designed, told Henri how she'd love an excuse to go to the beach Saturday, and said she'd give him a call.

Jen walked away while looking at the card. "So, March 22nd," Greg commented to get Henri's attention off of Jen's retreating backside.

"Yeah, last March. I walked into Lois's Bliss Triangle as she calls it. Though I think it's more like a triangulation process than a place."

"Triangulation?" Greg asked for clarification.

"It's like surfing. You triangulate between points to find the sweet spot for the lineup."

Greg had a blank look, so Henri continued. "To find the right spot to catch waves, surfers will use two landmarks for positioning. Placed correctly in reference to the landmarks, a surfer will be in the right place to catch a break," Henri paused before continuing. "It happened here.

I was dealing with my mom and the end of my surfing career when this place became an escape for me. Bliss put me in the right spot to catch a break and start the next chapter in my life."

Greg tested Henri. "So, you're riding the wave of Bliss now?"

Henri smiled. "Happily on my way. Okay, maybe that sounds too out there for you." Henri took a drink. "Anyway, I took care of my mom after she had a stroke. I came here sometimes after she went to sleep. That's when I met Lois, and we talked a lot."

"Is your mom still alive?"

"No, she died last summer, a couple of months after my disappearance."

"I'm sorry for your loss."

"Thanks. It was a hard time all around. She was still recovering from her stroke when she was diagnosed with pancreatic cancer. The end was quick, five months in all, but it was still hard. I paused my life while I took care of her, so losing her made me face my own stuff again."

"What stuff?" Greg asked.

"My marriage and surfing career were done," Henri paused to take a sip of water.

"Surfing career, huh?"

"Yeah, my family traveled a lot, so I found a way to continue to travel through surfing. I worked on freighters to get passage between places: Europe, South Africa, the Seychelles, India, Thailand, and the like. You know."

Greg nodded.

"Then I rode an insane wave in Tahiti and was invited to surf Cloudbreak, in Fiji, for a tryout of sorts. I got sponsors from that and immediately flew down to Australia. It's a great gig if you can get it. That's for sure," Henri smiled.

Greg smiled politely.

"Third year on the tour, I met what I thought was a cool chick, things clicked. We got married at the stop in Tahiti. Things were good. But, the fifth year was bumpy. I

31

never found my groove. Then, at Pipe, I dropped into a wave, got pearled, and surfaced with a snapped Achilles.

"My wife and I stayed in Hawaii while I rehabbed. It took more than a year just to feel sure of walking without crutches or a brace. Turned out she was more into being with someone on the tour than being in love with me. A year and half after I left the tour, she left me and returned to the tour as someone else's shadow," Henri took a gulp of water to get the sour taste from his mouth.

"The day the divorce was finalized, one of my sisters called to say mom had a stroke. I needed to get back to California immediately," Henri let out a small sigh. "I took the first flight out. Her right side was the one affected. She lost the ability to speak clearly. She couldn't remember basic information like her children were, where she lived, or what bank she used."

"Sounds bad," Greg offered.

Henri nodded. "I stayed at her house the month she was in the hospital and then the three months in the nursing home. My sisters have busy lives in New England, so I got tapped to take care of mom. We had a nurse that visited a few times a week to give me a couple of hours off."

Jen came to check their drinks and see if they wanted to order.

Henri resumed when she left. "Don't get me wrong. I wanted to be there for mom, but it was a recipe for disaster. In taking care of mom, I let myself go. I grew a gut, a beard, and wore old sweats or shorts all the time. That's probably why Jen didn't recognize me," Henri pointed to Jen over at another table. "I stopped caring. Just showered, threw something on and went."

"Wow."

"No kidding," Henri nodded at Greg. "If I wasn't dealing with mom and doctors, then I was with mom and vegging in front of the TV at home. After two years of that, I started coming to Bliss when I could. Lois and I started talking. She told me how Phil died. She wondered how different life might have been if he had a survivable stroke.

32

Lois offered to sit with mom if I needed to blow off some steam, but I didn't take her up on it. Mom was my responsibility as I saw it.

"Early last year, mom was diagnosed with pancreatic cancer. She gave up the fight and shutdown," Henri shrugged.

"I'll never forget it. March 22nd was a Thursday, the doctor ordered mom back to the hospital. I snapped at the doctors and was told that I wasn't welcome back in the hospital until I could handle myself in a properly. I got here five minutes later. Lois was behind the bar. She talked me down from my rage, when I ran out of steam she gave me a hug. That alone took courage because I don't think I had showered in days." Henri smiled awkwardly.

"She told me that she understood how hard it is to lose a loved one, especially a parent and one you felt responsible for. Then she said it was probably for the best because it would allow me to get on with my life as well. She assured me that was what mom wanted. The place got busy, and I got up to leave. I remember hearing the chimes go off at the door because they sounded different. While that registered, I stepped through the door, and...

Sara's Original Backstory

Two days later, Greg resumed his sleuthing at Bliss. He avoided coming in to keep Jen off of his mind. A striking woman entered the room wearing all black, a big silver necklace, a belt buckle on her jeans and cowboy boots. Greg immediately took notice. She had long black hair and dark eyes. There was a power about her, without being masculine. Greg figured this had to be Sara. "Hi, are you Sara?"

"Why yes. Are you Greg?"

Greg nodded, and she slid into the booth opposite Greg.

"Thanks for coming. I'm sure you're busy leading up to the awards show. I appreciate the time." Greg was ready to go since Sara was due in Vegas that night. Jen came to the table to see if Sara wanted anything and gave a perturbed look at Greg who was fixated on Sara. He was amazed that the woman in front of him was the one Lois described, but Jen saw it as a different kind of interest. Jen let out a huff, and Greg distractedly added a request for a refill to Sara's drink order. With a look towards the sky, Jen turned on her heel to get the drinks together.

"I know you've got a tight schedule, so let's get going. As you know from our phone call, I'm researching a series of disappearances from Bliss."

Sara nodded to Greg and looked around the place as he spoke. "Mind if I ask a question?" Sara interrupted.

"Not at all."

"What made you start looking into these disappearances?" Sara paused. "I mean it seems so random. I know that I haven't talked much about mine."

"I read about Mikel Thomas's disappearance and wondered how he could go missing without it making the news."

"Mikel Thomas. Why does that name sound familiar?"

"He was a basketball player that died a few weeks ago," Greg replied.

The light dawned on Sara. "Oh yes, he was interviewed the night he died. I was one of the other guests on the show that night," Sara grimaced. "It was an awkward moment. Felt like I was dropped in the middle of a spat."

"You were there?" Greg forgot that Lois mentioned the situation to him earlier.

"Yep. It was sad to find out he was dead hours later."

"No doubt," Greg brought the discussion back to Sara's experience. "I know your disappearance occurred July 3, 2012, right?"

"Yes. I call it my personal Independence Day," Sara laughed and thanked Jen for her drink. "It's been over a year since I've been here. Got to be a regular here for a while. Is Lois around?"

"Don't think she's in right now. Haven't seen her since I got here. She's the one who told me about your disappearance. Technically, she told me that you had an experience but didn't talk about the details. Says you simply left for greener pastures."

"Greener pastures are, in my case, Nashville of all places," Sara chuckled. "If you knew me a couple of years ago, that would be the last place you'd think to find me."

"Can you tell a little about what led up to your disappearance?"

"Well, I grew up a few towns away. I was more musical than academic, so I spent most of my teen years playing around with bands." She paused for a drink. "In high school, I met Tim, and we were on-again, off-again boyfriend and girlfriend throughout high school. We ran in the same circles."

"Instead of college, we tried our hand at getting a record deal. We were young and full of ourselves. We thought how hard could it be? Really, our music was all over the place. One hot mess describes it all," she laughed loudly. "Seriously, the name of our band was One Hot Mess."

Greg laughed. "Name says it all, huh?"

"Indeed, the music was schizophrenic, and life got down right insane quickly. Tim wanted to do harder edged music, closer to speed metal. The entire band shared a horrible, studio apartment in Silverlake. Four guys, me, and random girlfriends slept wherever we could. We survived on Ramen and cereal. It's the kind of thing you shake your head about when you look back."

Jen stopped at the table to check on them and gave Greg a look.

"Anyway, things got tiresome for me right as we caught a break. A talent scout heard our demo. Long story short, we were signed to limited and highly unfavorable contract with a sketchy record label. The guys decided the band was going in the direction of hard and fast musically. They hired a new guitarist. There was no room for a chick in that kind of band, so I was given heave ho." She let out a huff. "I was long-legged, big-boobed, and edgy. They loved having me around, but I was nothing but a glorified groupie at that point.

"Somehow, by dumb luck or what have you, a talent scout for a major label heard them play one night and had them come into the office the following week. The rest, they say, is history. You know the band Dark Star?"

Greg nodded. "Not my kind of music, but I have a few friends that like them."

"Well, Tim is Zaxson, the lead singer. They hit it big, and I played the dumb, dutiful girlfriend. That was until we decided, during a trip to Vegas, to tie the knot in one of those cheesy Elvis quickies. We thought it was hilarious. Days and nights were a blur of drugs and alcohol, so it was hard to take anything seriously. By then we were partying out of control. The money rolled in, and everyone bought their houses and sports cars."

"They toured nearly two years straight. While they were touring, I was told which concerts I could and could not go to. If they were nearby, Tim would send one of his "personal assistants", as he put it, to come babysit." Sara did the air quotes with an added grimace. "No doubt, there were parades of ready and willing women being had by all."

Sara paused to take a drink to get the sour taste out of her mouth.

"That life was exciting for the first year. By the second year, the road was starting to have an impact on everyone. After that, the spiral began. The drummer overdosed twice in the month the second album was released. Then he was involved in a terrible car accident. Tim was involved in a weird pyrotechnics accident at a festival near Palm Springs, and the band was forced to take four months off while he recovered.

"During those four months, we were forced to face each other for the first time. Let's just say, no good can come from having two virtual strangers forced to play house in a drugged out, cash rich fantasy. Tim didn't handle the burns well and added prescription drugs to his daily cocktail of crazy. While I changed his dressings and tried to keep the house, he hired a bevy of 'nurses'". Sara did the air quotes again, "and brought the 24/7 party into our living room."

"Sounds intense," Greg stated.

"Yeah, it was. One night he got out of control when I said we needed to put the party on pause. We came to blows, and I ended up knocked across the living room. I called the cops," Sara sighed.

"Money talks. He paid a fine, saw an anger management counselor, and did some community service announcements while cutting off all my access to money. My credit cards were taken away. My car was taken to the dealer and replaced with a Mercedes that I didn't get keys to, and so on. I even got my own personal assistant, who was no more than my keeper." She paused for a drink and then added, "Tim put me in my place for creating bad press."

"What happened to the idea that any press is good press?" Greg asked.

"No kidding. Especially with a rock band, but that's when I began to spiral. I was nearly locked down in my own house with someone who went between crazed and just plain despising me. My family wasn't around. We hadn't talked in years because they didn't approve of my choices. Friends from high school had moved on in life, and friends from that chapter in life weren't friends at all, just hunting celebrity. I didn't think I had anywhere to go and had nothing to fall back on.

"After a few months, I was broken. I skimmed his pain killers to deal with the injuries. I started to stop in here on my walks even though he paid someone to tail me all the time. It was the only place that the guy let me be for any length of time. I guess he was showing some weird sort of mercy.

"The third or fourth time I came in Lois was working the bar. She noticed the black eye behind my sunglasses but didn't say anything. I had a drink, and she left me alone. When I was ready for my second, she slipped me a card. It was a card for a battered women's shelter. I started crying and couldn't stop.

"I cried through my second and third drink. Then she refused to serve me. She told me that there was help for me, but I didn't believe it. Lois even offered to take me to the shelter herself, but I refused."

Sara took several breaths, and Greg let her be.

"That night I went home and left the card on the dresser. It ended up in Tim's hands. He flew into a rage, and I ended up with two black eyes, a split lip, and a fractured rib."

Greg winced and sat back in the booth.

"Two days later, I went for a walk, and my shadow told me to get in the car when I got around the corner. He asked if I had any friends. I laughed and told him the only friend I had was the bartender here. He drove me here. I got out and never looked back."

Greg understood that there were parts of the story she wasn't sharing.

Sara worked to get out of the bad place her memories had brought her back to. She took a drink. She looked around. She stopped to be thankful that she wasn't that girl from just over a year ago.

"I walked in here early that day. Lois wasn't behind the bar. It was some other guy. I sat and drank and drank and drank. I sank into my hopelessness when Lois entered with a big hello and a bigger hug. I cried out because of my hurt rib, and she got mad. She lectured me and told me how I could fix the situation. I was drunk and scared enough that I just fired back. She kicked me out. I stormed out the door and turned around to slam it, but the door was no longer there..."

Richard's Disappearance (Original Version)

Greg walked into the office to find the bright glare of white walls and fluorescent lighting a bit overwhelming. A sign greeted Greg:

MATTHEWS AND JENNINGS
Partners in Your Financial Future

Otherwise, the main office had the usual waiting room chairs, a receptionist's desk, and three doors to smaller rooms. Greg returned the greeting from the college-aged receptionist and told her that he was there for an appointment with Richard Matthews. She nodded and motioned to a chair while she called him.

A man in a charcoal gray suit and thinning brown hair came out of one of the rooms. "Hi, I'm Richard. You must be Greg,"

Greg stood to shake his hand and nodded.

"Come with me." Richard shut the door behind Greg. "Lois told that you might be calling. So, you are looking into the disappearances, huh?"

"Yes. Thank you for taking the time to talk with me." Greg took the seat Richard gestured towards and got out his notepad and voice recorder.

Richard took off his jacket. "I don't like to think about my disappearance much." He sat down in his large desk chair. "Don't get me wrong. I'm thankful for the wakeup call, but the whole thing was unnerving. I ended up dealing with some bad stuff."

"Not a good experience?" Greg asked when he was settled.

"In the end it worked out okay, but that time - in whatever reality that was - definitely wouldn't be something I'd revisit. I learned an important lesson though."

"What?" Greg asked.

41

"Money can be viewed two ways," Richard said intently. "It can be used as a tool for good," he chuckled, "or it can make you simply a tool."

Greg smiled. "You disappeared on March 19, 2011, right?"

Richard nodded.

"I've talked with others who've disappeared," Greg continued. "The disappearances seem to be tied to what's going on at the time. Could you give me some background on how life was for you then?"

"My trip, if you will, falls in line with the others in that case," Richard leaned back in his chair. "Let's see it probably goes back to 2001. My wife and I lived in Manhattan. I had a solid investment job with a major international broker. My wife was a freelance photographer. Times were good. We moved in powerful social circles. We were so busy that we had put off having kids."

Richard's voice changed in line with giving an extended explanation. "In finance, in New York, there's a lot of networking and information sharing that goes on outside of the office, and my wife was very understanding. There were periods of time where we were like two ships passing in the night rather than husband and wife. Often, the firm would entertain foreign heavy weights who wanted to live it up while in the States. That meant big meals, lots to drink, and other shows and entertainment...if you know what I mean," Richard looked at Greg.

Greg nodded. "I get the picture."

"My wife had a big showing at a posh studio on September 10, 2001. I forgot and went out with clients that night. We were out until sunrise. Several of the girls from the clubs showed up on the floor my clients secured at the Waldorf. Then other girls came too. Let's just leave it at that."

Richard's voice returned to a storyteller tone. "I walked into our apartment, figuring that Cynthia would still be asleep, but she wasn't. She was sitting on the couch.

Normally, she's not the type to make waves. This time she had guns blazing."

"We were having the biggest fight of our whole marriage. The proverbial kitchen sinks were tossed in both directions. Every time I told her that we needed to table it until that night because I had to get to work, she'd start a new tirade."

Richard took a deep breath. "Moments later, all hell broke loose as the first plane hit the World Trade Center. Nothing was on TV yet. We were close enough to see the towers collapse from our windows later. My office was in Tower One. When that went down, I was sick. Any other day, I would have already been into work for a good couple of hours. I hadn't taken any days off of work in the years I had worked there. Talk about a wakeup call." Richard paused at the gravity of the situation. He knew that he was lucky to be alive.

"For the next few weeks, Cynthia and I were in a state of shock. We forgot our fight. We found excuses to be out of town and eventually, leased a place on Cape Cod while the company worked to reassign people and reestablish operations. We stayed at the Cape until the holidays. After, we came out here for Christmas and New Years and never moved back."

"I went into real estate then. Real estate was looking better than working with the stock market after 9/11 anyway. Cynthia quickly got work in the fashion and entertainment arena out here. Things returned to normal: good incomes, growing careers, busy social calendars, and so on. It was like we'd hit a do-over button."

"Then 2008 hit. The real estate market caved with the economy. By then, I had a side gig as a location scout for the film studios. Business slowed to a crawl when it came to buying and selling. Cynthia worked more to make up the difference, but she got pregnant. It wasn't an easy one. I retreated to the computer, but it wasn't for business. If you get my drift?" Richard eyed Greg.

Greg just nodded.

"I started to scout more locations for projects and found that my major accounts were tied to adult entertainment. One day, I was invited to sit in on a shoot. Every guy's dream, right?" Richard laughed. "I went to more and more film shoots. After all, the San Fernando Valley was the adult film capital. My escape became an obsession just as my family needed me most."

"On one of the shoots, I talked with one of the stars who explained how the business worked. A few thousand for a day's work sounded good. I was in good shape, still had my hair," Richard laughed again.

Greg mustered a tightlipped smile. *Where's this going?* He thought. *I'm afraid to ask. At least he's on a roll.*

"I made some calls and was scheduled for a 'go-see'," Richard made air quotes and looked at Greg. "You've gotta love that term. I walked in; got a once over by three people sitting behind a collapsible table in a rental office; was told to take off my clothes; and was told to show them what I had. Some screen test, huh?"

Greg nodded. He did not want to say a word.

"I was deemed...well-endowed and put on a casting list. Two weeks later, we were short on the mortgage and car payments, and I got a call. I was on set the next day. You'd think it was every man's fantasy, but it was far from it. Everything is choreographed to smallest detail and shot and reshot numerous times. The whole time you have a group of Teamster types watching your every move. The girls were either barely legal or beyond worked. As the male you're hired simply to be a tool, literally. Get it up and keep it up. That's it. It's not about getting off for the guy. In fact, if you do get off, it can ruin the shoot because of the lag time."

Greg's phone rang, and he rushed to dismiss it. "I'm sorry. I thought I turned it off."

"No problem. It happens. Anyway, I did three scenes that day. Got a check for about two grand after taxes. For six months, I continued to tell my wife I was

44

scouting behind the scenes when I was really in front of the camera. I didn't have any guilt because I convinced myself it was about being the breadwinner. When I felt any guilt, I'd stop at Bliss before going home and pound some drinks before going home to play the husband and father role." Richard stretched in his chair.

Greg shifted in his seat.

"It escalated when Cynthia was pregnant with our second. The more deviant the activities. The better the pay. The actresses got younger. Then after one real bad shoot, I stopped at Bliss to make it go away. I got loud and obnoxious. Became true to my name...a real Richard."

Greg and Richard both laughed.

"Lois got fed up with me and kicked me out. I tripped on the way out the door, and...

o8o

Richard landed hard against a wall. The room was dark, and the ground felt cold and wet. He didn't catch his breath before the first kick hit him hard in the kidneys. Then there was a blow to his head. Warmth flowed into his eyes as a fist slammed him in the mouth. His lip was split and two teeth landed on the ground. He tried to get up and felt hands clamp around his hips. He was bent over, feeling unimaginable pain when the unthinkable happened. He cried out into the dark room. Over and over again he cried out. The only response was a wicked laugh followed by, "Had to see if you take it as good as you give it."

Fighting to get away wasn't working, and Richard was only getting more disoriented with the struggle. Then the light flicked on. A figure with a stick charged towards Richard and his attacker. His attacker grunted a couple of times before they separated. Richard fell to the floor without fully recognizing the humiliating position he had been found in.

That realization didn't happen until the next day. Again, the darkness gave way to light, but this time it was

Richard opening his eyes in the hospital ward. His left eye was swollen, so he only had a partial view of the world he was in now. He wanted to touch the swollen eye but found his left wrist handcuffed to the bed. He felt disconnected from the reality of the situation and closed his eyes again.

A man in a white coat came in. He checked Richard's chart and checked his pupils. "Why am I cuffed to the bed? On my stomach?" Richard was coherent enough to ask.

With a huff the doctor stated, "You'll be like that until the stitches are out. Painkillers must be working if you can't feel why you're like that. I'm sure your memory will return when your concussion passes." The doctor pulled back the sheet covering Richard and did a brief examination of the stitches. He put the chart back in the holder and moved to the next patient. Richard saw a guy in the bed next to him and turned his head to see another occupied bed on the other side. A uniformed officer stood near the door.

Day turned to night and back into day. There were only two things that broke the monotony: hospital staff doing their regular checks and the heckles from those in the other beds. When the officer was in the room with a staff member all was quiet except for exchanges with those being examined.

Then clamor started again. "Taz shoulda finished you off," growled the prisoner on the left.

Two others added, "You're disgusting. Sick and twisted! Sick and twisted!"

From the right came, "the world would be a better place if you died."

Then a chorus of shouts, "this is cruel and unusual!"

It continued every time the door slammed and bolted shut.

Halfway through the second day, a man came in with an officer and wheeled Richard to a different room. When Richard's gurney cleared the door, the men left behind cheered. The officer yelled "Shut up!" as he slammed the door closed and locked it.

Richard was left in silence in the other room. He was checked and ate on his side. Darkness fell. He slept like he hadn't slept in months. Staff woke him up for checks, but the deep sleep returned as soon as the door locked shut again.

The third morning, the door opened, but instead of a staff member in scrubs, a man with dark hair, blue eyes, and a strong jaw stood with the uniformed officer. The man in the polo shirt and jeans walked to the side of the bed. The officer announced to the man, "This is inmate 147839. The one attacked in the shower three days ago."

"Hello, I'm Phil from Universal Prison Outreach."

Richard didn't say a word.

"I am part of a program to help counsel and rehabilitate inmates."

Richard remained silent.

"I am here to talk with you about the incident or anything else you would like to discuss. I am not a lawyer. I am not here in a legal capacity. Is there anything you would like to talk about?"

"Why am I here?" Richard said after some more silence.

"You were attacked in the shower," the man answered plainly as he slid a chair over.

"No, why am I here...in prison?"

"Mmm, you've been held on several charges, the type that put you at the bottom of the food chain, even in prison," Phil's stared at the prisoner. "You're here because you can't post bail. It's high because of the number of counts. Judge sees you as a flight risk."

"What! How?" Richard's brain short circuited. "Everything was legal."

"The studio you worked for got busted for some, um, questionable practices. You were the one who acted in them. You're a producer too."

"What?"

47

"First of all, you might want to know that it's September 10, 2011," Phil said and went silent.

It escaped Richard.

Phil followed up, "What's the last date you remember?"

Then it clicked. "March 19th, so it can't be September 10th now." *Why is this jerk off messing with me?* Richard thought.

"You know, my favorite poem is by Robert Frost," Phil smiled before starting.

"Two roads diverged in a yellow wood,
And sorry I could not travel both
And be one traveler, long I stood
And looked down one as far as I could
To where it bent in the undergrowth;

Then took the other, as just as fair,
And having perhaps the better claim,
Because it was grassy and wanted wear...

Richard interrupted. "I'm not in the mood or position for a poetry lesson right now."

"It's not about literature. It's about life," Phil stated. "No surprise such a stubbornly self-absorbed man finds himself in your position." He sat back and folded his arms.

"I didn't do anything wrong!" Richard said emphatically.

Phil roared with laughter. "You're in prison. That's what they ALL say. That is until it comes parole time. Then they claim forgiveness and want to be upstanding citizens again. Try another line."

"Seriously, I didn't do anything wrong. Last thing I remember is getting drunk. They kicked me out of the bar. Next thing I know, I'm getting attacked. I don't understand. I'd never do something truly sick."

"You sure?"

48

"Yes!" Richard shouted. *How dare you?* Richard thought.

"Was there a time where you thought you'd never sleep with someone other than your wife?"

"Yes."

"Was there a time you thought you would never be in the adult film industry?"

"Of course."

"You've done things you say you'd never do. What'd stop you from doing even worse?"

Richard was silent for a bit. "But that's just wrong."

Phil stayed silent.

"Sure, sleeping around and doing the films was not really moral, but they were legal."

"How did you justify it?"

"I was providing for my family." Richard shot back quickly.

"Really? How about the women during those nights in New York City? How about the women in the parking lots?"

Richard looked at Phil.

"Seems your moral compass has lost its needle. Is it too much to believe you found a way to rationalize more and more disturbing acts?"

"How do you know about the women? How can it be six months from what I remember? Is this some kind of trick? A sick dream?"

"Let's just say, as part of the Universal Outreach, I'm here to give you a wakeup call. Call it a dream. Call it a timeout. Call it a vision or hallucination, for all I care. You're standing at a crossroads. What are you going to do?"

"I'm not standing at all at the moment," Richard fired at the angel, devil, messenger, or whoever he was.

"Don't play semantics with me now," Phil said. "You must do something. Doing nothing is not an option because in doing nothing you are still choosing something." Phil paused to let the message sink in.

Richard stared at the floor.

"You know, I loved watching my dog chase squirrels up the trees in my backyard."

"That's nice," Richard squinted at the change of direction in the conversation.

"Think of it as a metaphor," Phil began.

"Are you saying I'm a dog chasing a squirrel?" Richard interrupted. "Think the saying is something about a dog chasing its tail. Not a squirrel," he added angrily.

Phil sighed, "Though you've been acting like a dog, in this example, you're the squirrel. Not the dog." He took a breath and began to explain. "There are myths and beliefs about a great Tree of Life. The dog symbolizes what brought you into this life. Karma. Whatever. Once here, the dog, in the form of challenges and choices you are presented with, chases you. Makes you move. When you start out on your life path, or in this case up the tree, it is broad and relatively easy to navigate. There's a large trunk. Then that single path forks into smaller, but still large branches. The branches get smaller. The challenges and choices you face, in this case the dog, pressure you as you make your way through the branches. You, as the squirrel can escape your problem by continuing up the tree, right?"

"I guess so."

"What if you, as the squirrel, find yourself on a branch that is too weak or leads to a dead end because of the choices you made previously? Are you stuck?"

Richard stayed quiet.

Phil waited him out.

Richard relented. "No. A squirrel can go back and find a different branch to run onto."

"Good." Phil smiled. "You can even jump from one branch to another and not have to retrace your steps." Phil paused. "Sometimes you have to trust a leap into the air, rather than retracing your steps, to get where you need to be. It depends on where you find yourself. You just have to focus on where you want to land, and you can change course in one move. There are times you've moved without understanding the lessons from your previous missteps.

Jumping without understanding what came before is as foolish as remaining stuck where you are."

The pair sat in silence again.

"It seems you have choices to make. Haven't your problems stemmed from trying to escape? In New York, you were escaping a passionless living situation through work. You left New York to escape the memories of 9/11. You started obsessing about women to escape your family's struggles. You started doing films to escape the fear of losing your lifestyle. You went to the bar after shoots to escape the feelings of guilt."

"How do you know all that?" Richard asked.

"Does it matter? Am I wrong?" Phil replied.

When Richard remained quiet, Phil continued, "The only person you can never escape in life is you. One of the tasks in life is to develop into the person you'd like to hang around with because, no matter what, you're stuck with you. When you become the person you like being around, others will automatically be drawn to you as well. Love yourself, and others naturally show up to love you too. Hate yourself, and others are pulled to you who lead only to your downfall."

Richard looked at the man. There was too much to process. *Have I hated myself the whole time?* Richard wondered.

"Listen, my time's up here. I do regular outreaches. We can continue to talk if you're still around, but quite frankly, I hope to never see you here again." Phil got up, nodded to the officer, and disappeared through the door.

The lock on the door clicked into place, and Richard was left to silence. Eventually, the flood of questions subsided. The sunlight from the barred windows faded, and he drifted off.

Greg and Jen's Steamier Love Scene

(Note: It's spicier than the final version, but it is still more of a PG-13 or R. Don't expect any 50 Shades type of action. It actually got even spicier in later drafts before being heavily edited for a "let the bedroom door close" situation.)

o8o

Before Greg realized it, the sun was lowering to the horizon. He checked the grandfather clock in Lois's living room and still had an hour before picking Jen up for their date. He still wasn't entirely sure how to approach things with Jen since Henri was still in the picture. After a little bit of thought, he figured he'd play it for what was worth and headed out for a quick errand. While he backed out of his parking spot, Jen came around the corner. He waved, and Jen put up her hands asking what the deal was. "I'll be back. Have a quick stop to make. I'll be over at 6:30."

Jen looked relieved. "Thought I was being stood up."

"Not a chance," Greg smiled and pulled away.

Fifteen minutes later, he pulled into his spot and bounded up the stairs. He shaved and took a shower before putting on a suit. He double checked his look in the full length mirror Lois hung in the hallway and turned to grab everything. Lois stood behind him.

"You look dapper tonight. Got a hot date?" She said slyly and adjusted his tie.

"Date? Yes," Greg regained his composure after being startled. "Jen and I are going out."

"Good."

Greg smiled. "We'll see how it goes. Don't wait up."

"You have a key," Lois looked like a happy mom. "Hope you don't need it. Have a good time."

"We'll do," Greg said as he shut the door behind him. *Feels like prom night.* He thought.

53

The commute was all of six steps. He knocked on the door of Jen's apartment and got a bark in return. Jen's faint voice told him to come in. He let himself in and handed Milty the first of the two items he held, a large bone. Milty attacked it with gusto. "That's for you," Greg patted the preoccupied pup's head.

"What's for me?" Jen asked as she came out of the bedroom.

"Oh," Greg lost his thought as soon as he saw her.

She wore a blue dress that fit tightly and showed off her tanned legs. It stopped his brain from processing words.

"These are for you." He recovered and held out a bouquet of flowers. She smiled. "I got that to entertain Milty while we're gone." He pointed to the dog happily chewing away.

"Thank you," Jen closed the distance between them, but instead of reaching for the flowers, wrapped Greg in a hug. "Thank you from both of us."

Greg returned the hug and felt a surge. He worked to keep the desire for more at bay. Jen pulled away and took the flowers into the kitchen. Greg hoped his enthusiasm wasn't as obvious as it felt. "Let me put these in water. Do you want a drink?"

"We've got reservations in about an hour, so I'll wait 'til we get there."

"Cool. Where are we going?"

"It's a surprise."

"Really?"

"Really, so hurry up," Greg smiled. "It's gonna take us about that long to get there."

"Ok, ok," Jen laughed. "I'll get a move on." She finished with the flowers, grabbed her purse, patted Milty's head, and followed Greg out the door. As they got to the top of the stairs, Jen tugged on his arm. "Thank you again for the flowers. I've never had a date bring me flowers." She hugged him, and Greg had to focus on getting down the stairs to the car.

Traffic wasn't half as bad as it normally would be during rush hour, so they made it to Pacific Coast Highway quicker than Greg thought they would. The last glimmer of daylight faded to orange on the horizon as they drove up the coast. It took about fifteen minutes to make it to the restaurant overlooking the ocean.

Greg learned that their table would be ready shortly, so they went to the outdoor patio for a drink. The sunset made the sky a brilliant orange. The server presented a bottle of wine, and Jen and Greg settled into conversation.

"So, remember our deal?" Greg said after taking a drink.

"What deal?"

"We'd have to be more adventurous the next time."

Jen hesitated. "Yeah, we'd leave pizza and barbeque behind. I'd never guess sushi along the beach though." She held up her glass in a toast. "To creativity."

"Cheers," Greg affirmed.

They touched glasses.

"This is really good," Jen stated after a sip.

"Glad you like it." He wanted to ask about Henri, but he didn't want to lose the mood either.

"This is way upscale from what I'm used to. Have you been here before?"

"Once. For my mom's birthday. Dad was away, so she needed a special treat."

"You get along with your mom well then?" She took another sip.

"Yeah, she's more understanding than dad. Dad's all about his career. She doesn't judge people like he does."

"Even though you've got problems right now, it sounds like you have a pretty solid family."

"It could be a lot worse."

"Trust me, it could. Dad left my mom when she was pregnant with me. We lived with Grandma until I was in fifth grade. Grandma was my rock. Mom did a lot of dating. One day she said she found 'the one', and we moved to North Carolina." Jen wrinkled her nose. "He lasted about six months. Then the string of men started over again." She sighed. "Mom got pregnant with my brother when I was in high school. Mom eventually married that man. It lasted three years. By then, I was out of the house, and they were a different family."

"Made it easier to get your own life though, right?" Greg asked.

"Not sure about the easier part, but it make me get out on my own as soon as I could."

Greg could tell that Jen wanted to change the subject. "How's the school search going?"

"Good actually," her relief was apparent. "I think I found the program I want to go with. It's mostly online, so that helps with keeping money coming in. It's more expensive than the state schools, but I'm guaranteed to finish in a year." Jen shrugged. "There are some loan forgiveness programs I can apply for too. That would be a big help."

The host walked up to them and showed them to their table.

"Everything's coming together for you then?" Greg asked.

"Hope so," Jen said as Greg pulled out the chair for her. It was the most private table in the restaurant. "Wow, you pulled out all the stops." They sat between windows with an ocean view and a lit fireplace.

"Of course, we have to be adventurous, remember?" Greg smiled and said something else.

"What? Sorry, I missed that," Jen regained her composure after wondering about the adventures in store for the evening.

Greg leaned closer. "I asked if you wanted something in particular or if you just wanted to order a boat." She looked gorgeous in the low light. He tried not to let his own distraction show.

"A boat?"

"A boat is a bunch of different things put together. Like a buffet for two."

"That sounds fun," Jen smiled. "I've only had sushi a handful of times, and it's only been a roll or two."

"A boat it is then," Greg smiled and motioned to the waiter. Once he ordered, Greg filled Jen's glass. He held up his glass. "Here's to a new adventure."

"To new adventures," Jen's glass met Greg's as they locked eyes and smiled at each other. Both wondered if the other was feeling the same way.

Dinner went quickly and leisurely at the same time. They talked and ate. Sometimes the topics were serious, other times they were silly. "So, was it happily ever after, after all?" Greg asked as he poured the last of the wine in Jen's glass and motioned the waiter for another bottle.

"What?" Jen's eyes went from the glass to Greg.

"The book. Did they live happily ever after?"

"Oh, the book," Jen breathed. "Yes, Stephanie inherited the family's ranch. Daniel came to work as the foreman. Her ex turned out to be an arsonist. He set the main house on fire as revenge. Daniel saved her. They hooked up and lived happily ever after in Montana."

"Good to know. The genre's safe with another fairytale ending," Greg said with feigned gallantry.

Both wondered if there might just be the possibility of a fairytale ending in store for the evening. The moon hung over the water creating a silvery path to their table. As the waiter arrived with the second bottle of wine, they decided to split a dessert that sounded too good to pass up. While they waited, a couple a few tables over get engaged. They fell into a companionable silence.

When the dark chocolate cake arrived, Greg watched Jen take a bite and dance in her seat. "That is so8o good," Jen said in a throaty voice that sent Greg spinning again. "You've gotta try it." She motioned for him to take the bite off of her fork.

He complied and had to admit it was good.

She took a couple of bites then held her fork out for him again. When he took the last piece, Jen laughed.

Greg's gave her a puzzled look

Jen explained, "Oh, nothing. It's just that we're already sharing plates like an old married couple." She blushed.

They decided to leave but didn't feel like driving yet, so they gave the last of their wine to the newly-engaged couple and headed towards the sand. Jen kicked off her heels and waited for Greg to get his shoes off. The tide was rising, so the beach was a narrow strip. "Come on, we have to at least put our feet in the water," Jen chided.

Greg shook his head.

"Come on! It's a crime to be at the beach and not feel the water!" Jen cajoled as she jogged to the water's edge.

All Greg could do was roll up his pant legs and follow her.

"See doesn't this feel great?"

"Cold's more like it." Greg stopped behind her in ankle deep water. He could smell her perfume mixed with the sea air. He wrapped his hands around her waist without thinking. *Was it the push of the water, or did she lean into me?* He thought.

Greg's arms around her did more than warm Jen up. She felt the warmth inside and out. She took a deep breath to stop her mind and enjoy the moment.

Greg felt and heard the sigh. It was too much to take.

Greg spun Jen around and didn't think. He brushed her lips with his and felt her submission.

It made him hungrier.

He pushed for more, and she responded with a tighter embrace even as she melted into the kiss. The heat between them grew, and neither backed down. They both wanted and needed more. Greg thought about picking her up and tossing her on the sand.

A wave crashed into them. Jen caught her balance, but Greg fell backwards into the shore break. Jen laughed while Greg lay in the wet sand. "Guess one of us needed a cold shower."

Greg got up. "One of us?"

"Okay, *we* needed a cold shower. Let's get out of here before you catch a cold."

They ran to the valet. "At least I have a sweatshirt," Greg tried not to shiver in the cool sea air.

Jen laughed again, apologized, then laughed some more.

Greg tipped the valet, popped the trunk, pulled off the wet jacket and shirt and threw on the sweatshirt. "Ah, that's better. Wet pants are gonna bite though."

That sent Jen to giggling again.

Greg cranked up the heat before starting to laugh at himself. "Great impression, huh? You get me hot, and I wet my pants."

Jen laughed so hard tears came to her eyes. "I-I-I'll never look at you the same a-a-a-gain," she choked out between laughs.

"Wonderful," Greg said good-naturedly.

Jen still fought to control of her giggles as she reached for his hand. They drove back, hand in hand, in a combination of laughter and silence.

Greg pulled into his parking spot, still in his uncomfortably soggy pants. He came around the car to get Jen's door, and held out his hand as she got out.

Jen stood and slid her hand up his arm and around his neck. "If I remember right, I still owe you a movie," she said as she brought her mouth to within a breath of his. "How about you get out of those wet pants, and I'll see about a movie?"

Greg forgot about his wet clothes. All he saw was Jen, less than an inch away. He smelled her perfume and felt the heat of her body. "You want to go see a movie now?" His voice cracked slightly with his forced control.

"Who said anything about going to see a movie?" She paused and lightly kissed him. "I thought we'd see what was on TV."

59

"Okay." It wasn't profound, but it wasn't a time for thinking.

"Change and come over. We'll see if there's anything interesting on." She smiled and started for the stairs with her heels in her hand. Greg watched her move up the stairs before taking the stairs two at a time.

No thought was involved. He tore through Lois's apartment, threw on some jeans, and was back out the door before Lois could get a word in edgewise.

He didn't notice the grin on Lois's face or hear her laughing. "Ah, the chase is on," Lois mused before returning to her TV show.

Greg knocked and opened the door in a single motion. Jen had changed into a tank top shirt and shorts. She was in the kitchen area when Greg came through the door. "Howdy stranger," she smiled. "That didn't take long."

Greg crossed the living room. He pushed Jen up against the wall and kissed her.

She groaned, which just made Greg want...need more. She returned his passion with her own.

Greg picked her up and placed her on the counter.

She wrapped her legs around him as he pulled her in tighter. The kisses were deep and fierce. Jen dug her fingers into Greg's hair.

Greg's hand moved from her waist up under her tank top. His hand traveled up her back, and she moaned. The combination of her sound and the silky smoothness of her back gave Greg more of a rush as he realized there wasn't a strap in his way.

Jen took Greg's sweatshirt off in one motion. It went flying somewhere, and Jen's hands explored Greg's chest. She could feel his heartbeat. She could see his pulse in his neck. She wondered if her eyes looked as hungry as his. She wrapped herself tightly around him again with only the tank top between them.

Greg's lips began to travel as he tugged at her lip and then found the curve of her neck.

60

She raked her fingers across his back. "Let's go to my room," Jen said into Greg's ear.

"I need you now," Greg said, covering her mouth with another all-encompassing kiss.

"I know," Jen pulled away. "Let's go to the bedroom."

"Later," Greg replied. "Now." He pulled her into him tighter.

Jen realized they wouldn't make it to the other room. She nibbled at the throbbing point on his neck and knew that wasn't the only thing pulsating. As she teased at his neck, she undid his jeans and reached inside to massage his other pulse point.

Greg groaned.

She pushed her hands down between his hips and his jeans and let the clothing fall to the ground. The sight of Greg made her forget to breathe. She wrapped herself around him feeling the need even more.

Greg slid his hand under her and picked her up as his tongue probed deeper for hers. He held her in midair against him until he couldn't take anymore. He had to know her, have her. He pulled her down to straddle him. Slowly, Greg worked his way down her neck. His hand cupped her gently but greedily.

Jen closed her eyes and let her head fall back.

Greg lifted her tank top and pulled it over her head. He wove his fingers into her hair as his mouth found the first hardened point. His lips and his tongue teased at it, as Jen gasped and melted unto him further. When the first was attended to, he moved on to the second and sent a new wave through Jen. He took her hips in each hand and lifted her slightly to explore she soft quivering belly with his lips and then trace it with his tongue.

When Jen began to quiver, Greg laid her back and tugged off her shorts. He followed them down and then slowly, nearly torturously for both of them, made his way from her ankles to her knees, to her inner thigh and into her warmth. He wanted to feel and taste every part of her and enjoyed feeling her hit wave after wave of sensation.

Greg kept himself and Jen on the brink for what seemed like a glorious eternity.

"Now." She pulled at Greg.

"You sure?"

"Never wanted anything more," Jen said breathily.

That was all it took. Greg lost all control and took Jen in a hot and heated exchange what was primal and passionate for both of them.

"I'll never look at my kitchen the same way again," Jen said when they both got their composure back.

Greg laughed and helped Jen get up.

She kissed him playfully. "Want a drink?"

"Sure, I need to refuel."

"Does that mean there's another round?" Jen asked mimicking Greg's tone.

"Name the place and time," Greg took the glass Jen offered.

"Place and time, mmm," Jen eyed Greg over her glass. "Next time it's somewhere softer, and as far as time goes" she paused to take a drink. "When you're ready, I'm ready."

"Well then." Greg smiled.

"Well then." Jen acknowledged the challenge.

Reader Resources

After getting some of the background on *Triangulating Bliss* and the journey to publication, the time has come to explore the novel itself. In this section you will find a variety of information beginning with a synopsis of the plot. With the number of characters present in *Bliss*, the first section covers the cast of characters with brief descriptions to provide clarification. From there, a quick timeline for the disappearances in the novel is presented to keep things clear.

The final sections in the Reader Resources area include a list of discussion questions and topics that cover the novel, as a whole, as well as an author Q&A section.

Synopsis

(Note: In a traditional pitch to agents and publishers the synopsis covers every twist and turn in the story. Given that this is directed at readers rather than publishing professionals, this can be viewed more as a teaser summary rather than a classic synopsis...I don't want to take all of the fun out of reading the novel. There are also some bonus notes included regarding the novel.)

- What if you could take a complete time-out to figure things out when life got difficult?
- What if you could see disaster before it struck and be able to avoid trouble?
- What if you could share one more moment with a departed loved one?

All it takes is walking through the right door, at the right time...

Triangulating Bliss combines the magical, metaphysical, and mundane aspects of everyday living. It leads the reader to experience the joys and realities of life while illustrating that Einstein's beliefs about the fabric of time may not only be a part of the human experience but also the gateway to divine assistance.

In Pasadena, California, Greg Ellison is haunted by his experience in Afghanistan and realizes that life is too short to continue to live according to outdated expectations. His decision to drop out of law school and defy family expectations has consequences. Greg knows what he doesn't want, but he fails to understand what it is that he actually does want.

When he reads about the mysterious disappearance and death of a local basketball star, Greg is drawn to learn more. He meets the owner of Bliss, the business blamed for the death, and discovers that there are others who have "disappeared".

- The owner reunites with the love of her life and learns that love never dies;
- A woman, broken by life, sees how her life might be;
- A musician's wife stumbles upon her own grave;
- A son, caring for his dying mother, learns that endings can be beginnings; and
- A financial advisor with a shady past finds out how close he is to losing it all.

All of their stories include one figure...a man with dark hair, blue eyes, and a strong jaw.

Then, it's Greg's turn to face what lies beyond the door to Bliss.

Greg's encounter with the mysterious forces at Bliss changes everything. He learns that what brought him to Bliss is not as it appears and that the lives touched by the "Bliss Triangle" are powerfully interconnected across space and time.

Triangulating Bliss combines elements of a Nicholas Sparks story with a nod to classics such as *It's A Wonderful Life* and popular films like *Pay It Forward*. Hints of the magical in stories like *The House of the Spirits, Beloved,* and *The Alchemist* bring an added dimension to this tale of a quest to discover contentment with life amid loss and change.

Triangulating Bliss is a tale of living life to the fullest; but to understand, you must first disappear.

5 Points of Interest about the Book's Content or Story

Quantum Connections:

"Some things just ARE". Lois, the owner of Bliss, makes that statement when Greg first meets with her and challenges the nature of the disappearances. One of the fundamental prerequisites for Magical Realism to work as a genre is that the reader is willing to suspend belief or logic when magical or fantastical elements are introduced. However, scientists have worked to prove the fantastic may indeed exist in the form of parallel realities. The Fabric of Time is a concept of a four dimensional existence that Albert Einstein discussed in *Relativity* (1952). It states that the past, present, and future all exist at the same time. This mirrors the nature of the "Bliss Triangle" and what the characters experience during their disappearances.

Also, Richard Feynman used quantum mechanics to address the issue of multiple, simultaneous realities with his *Sum Over Histories*. The premise is that the reality a person experiences is only one of many possible directions time can take. Possibilities exist for all kinds of forward, backward, and sideways movement in time that manifest as alternative realities. If there is no sense of past or present, as Einstein argued, then Feynman argued that the sum of all possible histories leads to numerous space-time worlds co-existing at once.

Natural Connections:

Just like there are cycles to life where we sow effort and reap rewards or consequences, *Triangulating Bliss* uses the phases of the moon as a metaphor for what type of

69

guidance is needed and delivered. Both in folklore and the novel, new moons are often associated with beginnings and transitions. Full moons are associated with endings and manifestations. A full moon isn't just about acting crazy. It's when the moon is at its most powerful, so it magnifies what a person is focused on, positive or negative.

Novel Considerations:

The underlying premise of the novel is that in helping others, we help ourselves. When we concentrate on our hurt, our focus stays internal in an endless loop of suffering. When we focus, in a healthy way, on helping others through whatever gifts we possess, the loop is broken as we find purpose in life. Living with purpose is following your bliss to achieve happiness within your reality.

Bliss is a person, place and thing. Yes, in *Triangulating Bliss,* "Bliss" is all three. The goal of the characters is to find bliss (the concept or the idea) in order to be happy. Bliss also is the physical location, Bliss Bar & Grill, for the central elements of the plot and serves as a character, of sorts, in its own right. At the end of the novel, we are introduced to a final character that rounds out the trifecta. In this way bliss represents the overall story as human, physical, and magical.

Bliss Challenge:

Lois states, *"I always wanted to be a fairy godmother. It'd be great to do a little magic and make peoples' dreams come true."* One of my personal pathways to bliss is helping others through reputable charities. I became so close to the character of Lois that I hit a road block when preparing to write some of the last chapters of *Triangulating Bliss*. To honor the character that I came to love, as if she was really a part of my life, as well as a way to continue to "pay it forward", 10% of all proceeds from the sale of *Triangulating Bliss* and all funds from the companion guide *Backdoor to Bliss* will be donated to the Make-A-Wish (R) Foundation to help make the dreams of children and their families come true.

Character Sketches

Triangulating Bliss evolved into a much wider cast of characters than originally intended. I understand that it can be a bit overwhelming as a reader to try to remember all the introductions, which is why I typically try to limit my cast. To provide a little extra assistance, this section covers the characters included in the novel with some descriptions that supplement the text. There are a few characters, mentioned in passing, that are not part of this list. The deciding factor for inclusion in this discussion is that they play some sort of instrumental role in the overall story arc. It is broken into the categories of major, secondary, and sideline.

Major Characters

The most prominent characters in *Triangulating Bliss* are Greg, Lois, and Jen.

Greg Ellison: When the novel opens, Greg is working to redefine his life after returning from Afghanistan. He has been physically wounded as well as dealing with PTSD. Greg has lived his life according to "plan"…his dad's plan. He has hit a crossroads. After dropping out of law school, he learns about the suicide of a professional basketball player and begins to pursue his curiosity about the mysterious disappearance from Bliss Bar & Grill that is believed to be the cause of Mikel's death. During his investigation, Greg learns about important family secrets that change his perspective of life as well as finding out that Mikel's so-called disappearance is not an anomaly. During his pursuit to understand what happens in the Bliss Triangle, Greg has his own experience. The experience becomes the ultimate life changer for Greg.

Lois Atwater: As the owner of Bliss Bar & Grill in Pasadena, California, Lois is the key to Greg's investigation of the mysterious disappearances. Previously, she moved from Chicago to Pasadena to further her career in physical therapy. Once in California, she met Phil and opened her own practice where one of her clients was

Mikel while he recovered from an injury in high school. Lois took over Bliss after her husband, Phil, died, and became the matriarch of her corner of the world, namely Bliss.

Jen Carlson: After relocating from North Carolina, Jen becomes an unofficial adopted daughter to Lois. She experiences the Bliss Triangle on the very first night she is in Pasadena. Her disappearance is the longest one of them all. Once Greg arrives on the scene, Jen takes an interest in both him and Henri.

Secondary Characters

The secondary characters play important roles in the development of the novel but are not at the core of the story. These characters are critical to understanding the nature of the Bliss Triangle and include: Phil, Mikel, Henri, Sara, and Richard.

Phil Atwater: In life, Phil was Lois's husband. In death, he is the 'Guardian of the Bliss Triangle' as the man with "dark hair, blue eyes, and a strong jawline." After meeting Lois in the late 1980s, he settles into running 'Our Place' (the name of Bliss before Lois took over). His "Phil-isms" are displayed at the door to Bliss as a testament to his role as an unofficial bar philosopher.

Mikel Thomas: His death is the triggering event that causes Greg to learn more about what happens as Bliss. He was a professional basketball player with a troubled past, but Lois firmly believes that his death as nothing to do with Bliss and is not what it appears to be. During Greg's interviews, he learns that both Mikel and Lois are the only two people to report having more than one disappearing event.

Henri Nevin: After being injured on the pro surfing tour, Henri returns to California to help care for his dying mother. The combination of losing his career and watching his mother get worse, drive Henri into depression. His disappearance from the restaurant helps Henri find a new direction in life which brings him back to Bliss.

Sara Mc Mullin: Now a songwriter in Nashville, Sara grew up in Southern California. She married her high school sweetheart who turned out to be anything but sweet. Sara's encounter with the Bliss Triangle is dangerously close to an encounter with death, but is it is the only way that she can be sure to save herself.

Richard Matthews: Now a paunchy, middle aged financial advisor, Richard's account of his disappearance from Bliss provides Greg with a story that goes from 9/11 and New York to the seedy side of Hollywood. Ultimately, Richard becomes a surrogate father figure for Greg as he struggles to re-shape his life.

Sideline Characters

These characters could also be considered secondary in the view of many readers. The key difference in this case is the development of the character. They tend to serve a purpose in helping the story evolve but their personal descriptions, background, motivation, and such are not addressed. These characters include: Mr. and Mrs. Ellison, Raffy, Nisha Thomas, Kennan Wyatt, Tara Wright, and Pete.

Mr. Ellison: Greg's overbearing, career-driven father who has focused on Greg becoming a lawyer in the family firm, regardless of Greg's wishes. He is the "boogey man" voice in Greg's head when it comes to choosing a different path in life. His secret is what ties Mikel Thomas to the Ellisons.

Mrs. Ellison: Greg's mother reveals that there are some family secrets that tie Greg, Mikel, and Phil together.

Raffy: Rafael works as a spiritual advisor at Henri's Wellness Center in Manhattan Beach. He helps Greg understand some of the timing involved in the disappearances.

Nisha Thomas: Mikel's soon-to-be ex-wife who find's Mikel's body in their home. Her story just doesn't seem to add up for Greg. Her reputation precedes her (and not for the better). She has a talk show and has other business interests.

Tara: Greg's college sweetheart. Greg was going to propose to her just after graduating college. After a fight over dinner, Tara runs off and is killed in a shooting. Greg fights guilt over her death and finds out that she had an additional secret he didn't know about previously.

Kennan Wyatt: Nisha's PR guy and lover. He was to have been fired when Mikel learned of his affair with Nisha and some embezzling of funds, but he remains at Nisha's side.

Pete: Greg's Army buddy. They were about to complete their deployment in Afghanistan when the convoy they were traveling in was attacked. Pete didn't survive, but Greg did. Greg serves as the escort back to the U.S. for Pete's body even as he is recuperating from injuries.

Bliss Triangle / Disappearance Timeline

To assist readers in keeping the disappearances straight chronologically, a timeline of the major events in *Triangulating Bliss* follows.

2009:

- December 31 - (New Moon) Phil Atwater Dies

2010:

- September 23 – (Full Moon) Lois's First Disappearance
- November 21 – (Full Moon) Lois's Second Disappearance

2011:

- March 19 – (Full Moon) Richard Matthew's Disappearance
- December 24 – (New Moon) Mikel Thomas's First Disappearance

2012:

- March 22 – (New Moon) Henri Nevin's Disappearance
- May 5 – (Full Moon) Mikel's Second Disappearance
- June 19 – (New Moon) Jen Carlson's Disappearance
- July 3 – (New Moon) Sara Mc Mullin's Disappearance
- July 19 – (New Moon) Henri's Mother Dies / Jen Returns from Her Disappearance

2013:

- September 19 – (New Moon) Mikel Dies
- October 18 – (New Moon) Greg's Disappearance
- November 17 – (New Moon) Lois Dies

Discussion Questions

- Greg drops out of law school in an effort to claim his life instead of living according to the expectations of others. In what ways have you lived a life that wasn't "authentic" to you? Have you done anything to become more authentic in your daily life?

- Greg seems to have been driven by a desire to please in pursuing law school even as he doubted it. Is it a universal experience that children live to please their parents? At the start of the novel, Greg is in his late 20s, is it realistic that the need to please carries over into adulthood? Have you ever put your own needs and wants on the back burner for someone else's agenda?

- Greg learns about his parents' indiscretions early in the book. His mom talks about how parents don't want to disappoint their children by being human rather than heroic. What was it like for you to come to understand that your parents were "mere mortals"? If you have children, have you encountered a moment when your child realized that you are real rather than superhuman? Does that realization as a child or parent change the relationship between parent and child?

- Greg talks about the nature of fear regarding his decision to leave law school as not being real (just the boogey man taunting him)? Do you believe there are different degrees of fear? If so, is it the result of the situation or the internal feeling being experienced at the time?

- Greg was raised to plan everything out in his life in order to be successful. Are you a planner or a "pantser" who lives life as it comes? Have you ever behaved in a manner that went against your typical style? How did it work out?

- The sayings posted at the door to Bliss serve as an introduction to both the restaurant and to the character of Phil. Many of them could be viewed as canned or clichéd. What makes such statements both frustrating and enlightening? How do the "Phil-isms" reflect the development of the story throughout the novel? How do they reflect Greg's personal journey?

- While Greg waits to talk with Lois for the first time, he reflects on how buildings can hold so much history. In fact, Bliss essentially becomes a character of its own. Have you ever visited a building that seemed to have a life of its own? If so, what made you feel like that?

- Lois became dear to my heart while I was writing *Triangulating Bliss*. She became the type of person that I want to be when I get older: intelligent, young at heart, caring, and resilient. She's seen the dark side of life and still remains alive and present after her struggles. Do you have someone in your life that you look to as a model for your future self? If you had to describe yourself in 10, 20, or 30 years, what words or phrases would you use?

- Lois goes back and relives the day that she got engaged during her first disappearance, yet she still has the knowledge of experience, as well as carrying the hurt in losing Phil. Is there a moment in time that you would choose to relive? Why or why not? If you could change it by revisiting it, would you intervene (even if it meant some other things in life wouldn't come to be because of the changes)?
- How do the differences in Lois's two disappearances reflect the nature of life, grief, change, and maturing?
- Jen seems to be annoyed with Greg from the time she meets him at the bar. Later we find out that she immediately recognizes Greg as "the one" from her disappearance. Have you ever been in a situation where the next phase of your life is before you and instead of excitement, you feel a sense of fear or even hostility? How does Jen's initial reaction to Greg (given what we later learn) mimic the struggles Greg encounters with his decision about law school?
- There is a cruel, and be it somewhat comical, twist in the fact that Jen returns to North Carolina the very day she arrives in California to escape her previous life. Have you ever been in a situation where you felt you took one step forward and two steps back? How did it work out for you? What was the theme or lesson Jen had to learn from her experience in the Bliss Triangle? Are there any parallels to Greg's situation?

- When Henri shows up at Bliss, Jen is immediately interested in him, yet she knows she's ultimately going to be with Greg. Was there any hint of this turn of events in her "This is your life" film experience? Why do you think she pursues the chance to be with Henri? Have you ever pursued a Mr. /Miss "Right Now" or a "Right Now" situation in lieu of the perfect or "Forever" version? What factors into that kind of decision?
- Henri's disappearance puts him right back in his version of "paradise" (in the water). How does his disappearance experience parallel and diverge from the one Lois recounted about Mikel? Does your life experience reflect your circumstances, or is your life merely a reflection of your reaction and perception of events?
- Sara recounts her life before her disappearance as well as the actual event. Have you ever been in a situation that seemed hopeless or inescapable? If so, how did you turn things around? When a major life change has to be made, do you think it is completed due to an internal shift, outside assistance, or does there need to be a combination of the two for success to be possible?
- When Greg and Jen go out on the pizza date, they enter a bookstore and play a game. What three books (or movies) would you choose to represent the person that you are? Why?
- Throughout much of the novel, Greg is haunted with memories of both his would-be fiancée, Tara, and his Army brother, Pete. Have you experienced a major loss and had to navigate the grief? Have you experienced or know someone who has experienced

PTSD? Is it possible to have PTSD without having been in combat?

- Grief can make people act and react in surprising and odd ways. When we learn that Greg didn't attend Tara's funeral and instead left for the Army, does that make him a more sympathetic character or not? He states that he "couldn't save Tara" so he "went to protect the country"? Is that noble and heroic or is it a sign of weakness and immaturity? Have you experienced extreme grief in your life? In the aftermath of a loss, have you made decisions that you later questioned or regretted?

- Richard's Bliss Triangle experience screamed to be told as noted in the previous deleted material discussion. The original version was far darker and grittier than the final version. Does his character truly achieve a level of redemption in your eyes, or does he fall under the category of "once a sleaze-always a sleaze"? Is true redemption or rehabilitation possible for anyone? Have you given a friend or loved one a second chance at some point? Does everyone deserve a second chance?

- When Greg finally confronts his father about law school, it gets ugly with the admission that Mr. Ellison is not Greg's biological son. Does that kind of bombshell have the same impact on an adult child as it does in one's youth? What truly makes a father a dad or a mother a mom?

- Do you believe in coincidence, serendipity, or fate? Have you had any life changing experiences as a result of any of those phenomena? Was it any of these that led Greg to find out the truth about his life?

- During Jen's disappearance, she talks about everything being destined and pre-prescribed, but Phil reminds her that everyone has free will. Do you believe that certain things are "meant" to happen? Do you believe you can change your destiny?
- Greg returns to Bliss after confronting his father, only to have his world collapse further when he and Jen come to blows about the lawsuit. Have you been in a situation where you thought things couldn't get any worse and then something else surprises you and kicks you while you are down? If so, was it a blessing or just another lesson to learn? Have you ever reached a point when it all became "too much"? If so, how did you handle it?
- How does Greg's disappearance mirror those of the others he interviewed? What is the fundamental difference?
- How does Greg's disappearance help in solving both his personal life mysteries as well as those of his quest to understand Bliss?
- Phil's role in regards to the Bliss Triangle is similar to that of a guardian angel. Do you believe in guardian angels and help from the other side? Have you had any experiences with the supernatural?
- Lois is a cheerleader for the growing relationship between Jen and Greg throughout the novel. Why would she take such a role? Are there similarities between Jen and Greg's romance and relationship and Lois and Phil's?
- Lois seems to understand the end is near as the novel moves towards its end. How did her death make you feel? Was the Bliss Triangle due to Phil or did Lois have a hand in it all too?

- Do you believe in life after death? What was Lois's legacy? How did it impact the world around her? Does everyone leave an impact when they die? Why or why not?
- What are the themes of the disappearances? Do they reflect universal experiences we have as humans? Do we all truly share the same types of struggles and triumphs, even if the circumstances differ between people?
- In the epilogue, we come to understand that Bliss is a person, a place, as well as a thing (idea or concept). Lois always held fast that you should "always follow your bliss". How do you define your bliss? Are you following it or have you gotten distracted? If you've gotten distracted, what are a couple of simple ways you can begin to follow your bliss once again?

Q&A

The following section is a series of question and answers regarding the novel and the author, Janelle Jalbert.

The book is dedicated to your father. Can you tell us more about him and why you chose to dedicate it to him?

JJ: My dad, Jerry, was a passionate and voracious reader. Typically, he had 4 or 5 books going at the same time, covering topics ranging from the writings of monks from hundreds of years ago to the latest military mystery. He was responsible for my love of reading and writing.

He ran a mobile car repair business for more than 30 years where many of his customers became friends because of his warm nature and willingness to listen. He served in the Marines during Vietnam and lived according to the motto "Once a Marine, always a Marine."

I was the stereotypical daddy's girl and his mini-me in girl form. Some of my most cherished memories will be the moments that I shared with him talking about how *Triangulating Bliss* was developing as I did the original draft. He was diagnosed with multiple terminal cancers while I was writing the novel, and he passed 8 weeks later. One of my biggest regrets is that he didn't get to read it before he passed.

Is it true that Bliss Bar & Grill was inspired by an actual place?

JJ: There is no Bliss Bar & Grill in Pasadena, California. The idea for the story came to me while leaving Gus's BBQ in South Pasadena. There's a hint of the feel from Gus's in Bliss mixed with other places I have frequented. People have told me it is similar to Smitty's in Pasadena, but I have yet to check that one out.

Are any of the characters based on real people?

JJ: All of the characters are creations from my mind. As with many writers, there are some similarities that become apparent as the characters get rounded out. When I first wrote Phil, I modeled him on a cross between a friend of mine and my dad (with the reference to the eyes). It wasn't until months after the drafting and my dad's passing that Phil really showed up as my dad in fictional form.

As to the other characters, I shared a similar situation in life as Greg does to start the novel, which was likely a subconscious motivation for his character. The novel opens with Greg leaving law school, and I had left my PhD program a few months before the story idea came to me. I was also reorganizing my life throughout the Bliss process. Also, much of Jen's story parallels my experiences from college and my twenties, so that's a little personalized fiction.

I do want to clarify that Richard's story is pure fiction. I have had questions about that because of the inclusion of prison and the adult entertainment industry in his storyline. Nope, I haven't been to jail, and I have not had any part in the adult entertainment industry. I did go to college in the San Fernando Valley back in the day when the area was ground zero for the industry, so that gave me additional insights rather than direct experience. (Those from the area can understand that one.)

We never really get to learn about Phil's story in Triangulating Bliss. Why isn't there more about him?

JJ: At first, Phil was just the mysterious man with "dark hair, blue eyes, and strong jawline". Lois's discussion of their meeting was done later in the drafting as the novel came in a non-linear fashion. It was her character that filled in those gaps. The story is done from the perspective of what people from "this" side experience on the "other" side, so it didn't seem right to add a different angle with the large number of characters and plot twists.

After countless revisions, I began to get curious about the how and why behind Phil's participation. That's when I thought about a follow up book. It's only been very recently that his story has come to the forefront to be written. As of now, *Triangulating Self,* Phil's story, is in the early drafting stages. I'm getting really excited about how it is developing.

What's up with all the "Phil-isms" throughout the novel?

JJ: At first they were simply something Greg noticed as he walked into Bliss. I pictured a board with colorful sayings on it that would catch someone's eye. As the story developed, I realized that the sayings were part of Phil's character as a "philosopher/bartender". Then, the sayings that came up tended to foreshadow events in the story, like Phil was giving advice that characters needed without necessarily being part of a disappearance.

The funny thing is that if you read them they are often clichéd expressions. I got some flak for that, but isn't that part of the magic or irony of life? We all want to believe that we are unique, but we all share many common experiences that are encapsulated in these reflections that can be seen as trite by the more cynically inclined.

What are the chimes all about?

JJ: Again, that was a revelation that came from Lois's initial chat with Greg. I didn't go into it with the idea of chimes ringing in a special way when a disappearance was imminent. When she explained that she put them up to help understand the disappearances, it made sense since there would be some who wouldn't return to confide in her about what occurred. As *Triangulating Self* takes shape, Phil has let me in on some of the background with the chimes, so that will be fun to share in the near future.

Why does the story end with the additional Epilogue instead of just ending at the Housewarming Party and engagement?

JJ: The novel could very easily end with the New Year's gathering and remain a satisfying experience. However, even before it became clear that Lois was going to leave before the story's conclusion, I had the hint of the ultimate ending involving Greg realizing that he had indeed found his own bliss, though he hadn't really known he was chasing it the whole time. That came in the form of a baby, and it also rounds out Jen's character as literally coming to full term with the child, unlike her previous pregnancy.

Who's your favorite character?

JJ: Hands down, it's Lois. I just came to love her so much. She has class and spunk with the blend of wisdom and being young at heart. I hope I'm like that when I get into my golden years.

Conversely, the character that gave me the biggest challenges was Greg. Part of it may have been that he was originally cast as a pseudo-me, and getting real about yourself in your writing can prove challenging. Numerous drafts (and I mean more than a dozen) still had me questioning if he came through as an authentic male character. It literally took a year and a half and new twists involving his college sweetheart, his parents' secrets, and diving more into his PTSD to find the right balance between confused and searching versus "wussy" and flaky.

What's your favorite part of the book?

JJ: Good question. There are several snippets that I really enjoy. I love the way Lois comes to life in the opening chapters. I laugh at Jen's banter during her disappearance as well as the date that ends with soggy pants. Seeing Bliss in the final lines is also heartwarming.

When it came to writing, the disappearances themselves flowed easily with the exception of second events for Lois and Mikel. Those were not as quick to develop. Surprisingly, Richard's shady tale was the one that screamed to be written first. That's when I knew the original idea of walking into a "perfect life" wasn't the direction everything would take.

Was any part of the book difficult to write?

JJ: The story really did come together surprisingly easy, even when the previously mentioned sections bogged down a bit. The difficulty wasn't the writing. It came when I knew I had to finally let Lois go. I knew it was coming and didn't want to see her go. Writing the fundraiser scene was hard just because I knew what came next. I actually stopped drafting for two weeks as I came to terms with it. I have to admit…I cried through all that and didn't fully recover until after the memorial service.

Why was the point made that people who experience the Bliss Triangle are regular customers at Bliss?

JJ: Part of that was the author interjecting herself. I could see readers dismissing it all as drunken escapades, so Lois brought up the point that the people who experience the Bliss Triangle are known and loved. There's a purpose to the disappearances.

What do you believe is the true nature of the people's disappearances?

JJ: Good question. I believe that there are things that happen that can be characterized as "unexplained". I believe that if someone truly believes something happens (not as part of a mental illness or other impairment), then it doesn't matter if anyone else sees it as rational or irrational. Is it possible that the people were somehow supernaturally abducted? I don't have all the answers about the supernatural, so I can't say yes or no. Were they dreams or hallucinations? Possibly. I tend to agree with Phil and Lois...some things just ARE. It doesn't matter if you understand all the mechanics behind it. All that matters is what you learn from it.

Why are some disappearances happy while others are sad or even disturbing?

JJ: Seriously, it was the characters who decided that. The original premise was all disappearances would lead to "Happily Ever After" scenarios. Then too, there wasn't a plan that the disappearances would be temporary in nature. Mikel's story was initial set up to be the anomaly where he returned and met with his demise back on this side. As I listened to the characters, I found out that was not the case. I guess it was all a matter of what the characters needed at the time.

You keep talking about the characters "telling" you things? Do you really believe that they are the ones talking?

JJ: It can seem odd to those who don't write to hear authors talk about characters taking control of a story. It may not happen for every author, but it does for me. I love it too. It helps me believe that the eventual readers will be similarly touched. It's the type of experience that is really why people continue to read books.

Even when I have a general outline for a project, the characters will often send it in new directions through the course of their conversations and actions. For example, when Greg and Jen have their beach date, it happened. I knew they were going to go on a date and where they were going. That was it. I even told my dad that as I prepared to sit down and draft it. I had no idea that Greg would end up with soggy drawers or that they'd actually get together that night. It's kind of fun that way.

How many drafts did you do of *Triangulating Bliss*?

JJ: Geez. I stopped counting after seventeen. I did seven in the first few months before diverting to another project for 6 months. I returned to it and did 10 more, swearing I was done. I've probably done another 8-12 in the months leading up to the release. There's no such thing as a final edit or being done. Writers know that there is always something that could be changed. You just have to make the decision at some point to get it a good as possible and let it be free. Otherwise, it will never see the light of day or eyeballs of readers.

Is your writing paranormal, supernatural, Magical Realism, or what?

JJ: I, personally, prefer to think of my writing as Magical Realism. It's a genre that big publishers tend to shy away from because they think it doesn't sell. I think that's hilarious because I find stories all the time that celebrate the "every day magic" of life. Paranormal is popular right now, but it has been dominated by werewolves, vampires, and zombies which doesn't gel with my writing even though the genre can include ghosts and supernatural phenomena. I like to think of my stories as being grounded in daily life while having magical elements. Magic doesn't necessarily mean witches, potions and spells either. It can include the synchronicities and serendipitous circumstances that arise in the form of signs and coincidence as much as it includes more spiritualized elements. I don't see it as conflicting with any religious traditions. Instead, the magic my writing celebrates is more of a recognition that what is perceived as "magic" is the manifestation or proof of the existence of a higher power.

What's your writing background?

JJ: I knew I wanted to be a writer when I was 10 years old. I began writing serial stories for my classmates. They were one page installments tailored to each friend that went out a couple of times a week. My writing stalled in college as I transitioned to teaching (oh the frustrated author cliché, I know). While teaching I found a few projects to channel my writing into. I wrote *Success Skills for Middle and High School Students* as a spin off for a summer school stint I was teaching in 2001. A few years later, I used my business background to contribute a chapter to *Conscious Entrepreneurs.*

In 2009, I decided to try my hand with Examiner.com. I was working on a PhD in education and pitched a position as a graduate school examiner. It was designed to help my transition into college admissions counseling. Instead, a few months later I parlayed that into two positions covering motorsports first in Southern California and then nationally.

It wasn't until the idea for *Triangulating Bliss* hit me in September 2013 that I returned to fiction writing. That was when I truly and officially rededicated myself to writing. As I said earlier, Bliss was drafted in six weeks and then my dad died New Year's night (that was ironic given Phil's death on New Year's Eve in the book…indeed, that was written before dad's passing). Two months later, I began seeking out writing work. I started doing ghostwriting for blogs at first. Then I submitted a story to a Flash Fiction Magazine that was accepted within a week. They offered me a regular contributor position writing stories as well.

The momentum grew, and I pitched a book idea to a publisher on Easter Sunday, literally. The auto responder stated it would take about 10 days to hear anything, but 24 hours later I had a book contract. As I wrote *Wine for Beginners,* I also worked on a collection of stories, *Flash 40: Life's Moments,* which was published later in the year. Even with all that, I continued to do ghostwriting for the top businesses on the internet as well as small businesses and even wrote nearly a dozen nonfiction books for international clients.

You mentioned ghostwriting. Why would a writer be a ghostwriter if they get no credit for their work?

JJ: There are two reasons I do ghostwriting. One, I love writing. Two, I happen to like paying my bills. Yes, recognition is a good thing, but I also truly enjoy what a paycheck does for my day-to-day life. Many writers never really get anywhere financially with writing because they dream of fame, fortune, and being a best seller. I can honestly say I have been making a living as a writer, even if someone else's name is on the cover or featured in a bestselling list.

Plus, I love learning and teaching which works well in non-fiction writing. I have written on all types of things from personal development to spirituality to wine and travel to sex and relationships and even finance and computers. I would probably look like a crazy chick from a branding point of view if had my name attached to all the books I've written in so many areas, so in the end there is a bonus there for marketing purposes, I suppose.

What's your greatest accomplishment?

JJ: Mmm. I hate to think that my greatest anything has already happened. It kind of puts a downer on the future. Plus, there's so much to life that it's hard to say one thing is the ultimate thing. Some of the best things have been seeing my books published, traveling the world to see places on my bucket list, and doing my stint in motorsports. (After all, I had been a high schoolteacher in Southern California a year before I was working pit roads around the country.) That's just a sampling. I'm sure there's more to come as well.

What's on your "bucket list"?

JJ: I started making a bucket list about the same time I figured out I wanted to be a writer. Of course, they weren't called bucket lists then. I've made it a point to knock a lot of items off as I go and replace them with new ones. For now, the top item (or the most challenging to accomplish at this point) would probably be flying with the Navy's Blue Angels. I spent a lot of time on flight lines and at air shows as a daddy's girl, and that's one thing that I've always wanted to do.

What do you do when you aren't writing?

JJ: It depends. On 'normal' days, I do marketing for my writing as well as continuing my writing projects. I have other employment responsibilities to take care of too. Free time is often spent tinkering as a cook, chilling with loved ones, watching racing, playing with my pooches, and reading. Otherwise, I love to travel. I have a tendency to go on impromptu road trips with no warning and have been known to book plane tickets without notice.

Do you have any advice for aspiring writers?

JJ: There is plenty of advice out there for writers. Personally, I'd say a few things. You have to love actually doing the writing as well as loving what you write. You need a thick skin and a tender heart to survive and find success. Understand the difference between your passion and your project (that may mean that you write a draft for yourself before drafting one for publication). Read, read, read, read, read, and read some more. You can't write well if you aren't willing to read constantly. Finally, understand that being a writer/author is a small business. You will need to split your time and effort between being creative and being in business as a promoter, etc. If you just want to write without the business side, you won't find success, even with a contract from a big publishing company. You have to be a go-getter.

Is the Bliss Challenge just a gimmick?

JJ: No. I wanted to find a way to do something good with *Triangulating Bliss* that was about others and not my personal interests. I do not have any hidden agenda with the program. I love what they do and have no personal ties to the organization. Throughout my life, I have worked to include community based organizations in all of my endeavors. Readers can vote for the Make-A-Wish (R) program that receives donations from the sales of the novel, and updates are available on TriangulatingBliss.com to make sure that there is no doubt about the nature of the program.

What's the deal with TriangulatingBliss.com?

JJ: Originally, TriangulatingBliss.com was designed to be the website for the novel. Instead of using the website solely for book promotion, I saw it as an opportunity to build a platform that promotes the pursuit of happiness...not just the book. Let's face it, it is a universal desire to be happy, and life can make that more challenging than it should be. There are sections dedicated to discussions of happiness, finding and following your bliss, and dealing with the challenges in life. The novel is also featured on the website with excerpts, other information and opportunities as well as community projects such as the Bliss Challenge.

Do you really want to hear from readers?

JJ: Yes. I honestly like hearing from readers and fellow writers. There are times when I have to behave and steer clear of spending a lot of time on social media or email in order to getting writing done, but I do love getting to know people and sharing experiences. I may not be online all the time, but I do make it a point to read posts and emails. I also have a regular, fun newsletter that goes out. I encourage readers to sign up for it. I understand we all get tons of emails. 'Salesy' stuff is annoying, so I work to avoid that. The newsletter is a mix of fun pieces, behind the scenes peeks, tips and tools, guest interviews, and specials that only "Team Bliss" subscribers receive.

Do you have any new projects in the works?

JJ: I mentioned before that *Triangulating Self* is in the works. I call it a tandem book to *Bliss*. It's not really a sequel or a prequel, but it is Phil's side of the story. There's a small excerpt of it in *Triangulating Bliss* and an extended excerpt here in *Backdoor to Bliss*. I'll see what readers have to say regarding other possible *Triangulating* books.

Another book baby of mine is due out in the Spring of 2016. It is the tale of my Carolina boy, Goose. If you love dogs and books like *Marley & Me* and *The Art of Racing in the Rain,* you will love *Wing Dog: Soul Pup.* If you are interested in learning more, be sure to sign up for the "Team Bliss" newsletter to get exclusive sneak peeks, perks, and special offers available only through Team Bliss.

Team Bliss

Team Bliss goes beyond the novel, *Triangulating Bliss*. It is more of a movement to help people pursue happiness and follow their bliss. The world has more than enough information and discussion of the foibles and pitfalls in life, but we crave assistance in how to improve ourselves and our lives.

There is no magic bullet, as much as I like to celebrate the magic in daily life. This rollercoaster of life is far too complicated for a plug-and-play solution. There are billions of people current living their own experiences right now, and as a result, there are billions of paths to happiness and bliss.

It doesn't mean that seemingly bad things still don't enter our lives while we pursue happiness, following each unique version of bliss instead enriches our individual lives and the world around us. That's truly the rationale for Team Bliss…to help each other live a rich life, regardless of what it is or is not.

There are several ways to join Team Bliss. One, you can simply choose to live life to the best of your ability and aim to leave the world a better place in one way or another. In that way, you are your own team. You can also join the "Team Bliss Newsletter" for regular pick-me-ups and good news.

If you would like to reach out for either support or to lend a hand to others who are also on the same journey towards bliss, you can start by visiting:

TriangulatingBliss.com

It's not simply a book site. There are articles and discussions about finding your personal happiness and bliss. You can also contribute to the discussion by leaving comments and questions on topics. You can share your own experiences and insights by contacting Team Bliss, or you can even guest post on the website for a wider audience if you wish. Simply click on the tab labeled "Team Bliss" to learn more about that and other opportunities to participate and to contribute. While you're there, sign up for the Team Bliss Newsletter for fun and useful discussions on topics related to happiness, bliss, and life purpose.

The Bliss Challenge

The Bliss Challenge is unique to *Triangulating Bliss,* but it is also a part of the Team Bliss movement. The challenge started as a way to take the character that I came to truly love and adore, Lois, and extend her passion to serve as a "fairy godmother" in helping others.

It quickly became clear that there could be a synergy between bringing Lois's character to life by doing something to brighten lives and Make-A-Wish (R) programing. With the way that Lois treasured her special Grand Opening gift, it reinforced the fact that Triangulating Bliss could be a force greater than an interesting or entertaining read.

To be clear, the Bliss Challenge is not an officially sanctioned program through any Make-A-Wish (R) organization. There is no endorsement of the Bliss Challenge or the novel to be implied.

So, what *IS* the Bliss Challenge? The Bliss Challenge is a program that Janelle Jalbert created to lend support to programs making wishes come true for ill children and their families. The goal is to raise enough from the sale of the novel and this companion guide to grant at least one wish for a child through Make-A-Wish (R) programs in the United States. As of this writing, a single wish ranges from $6,000-$10,000 depending on the type of wish and location.

Janelle has committed to giving 10% of the proceeds from *Triangulating Bliss* and 100% of the proceeds from this companion guide, *The Backdoor to Bliss.*

Readers will be able to decide which program benefits from the Bliss Challenge funds by visiting:

TriangulatingBliss.com/Bliss Challenge

In voting for favorite characters, readers will be able to determine where the contributions go to Make-A-Wish (R), as follows:

Greg, Mikel, and Henri = Los Angeles, CA Area
Jen = Charlotte, NC Area
Lois = Chicago, IL Area
Sara = Nashville, TN Area
Richard = New York City Area

Progress towards granting a wish (or more than one) is also available on the website. Regardless of the level of funds raised, donations will be made annually beginning in December 2016.

A more detailed explanation of the Bliss Challenge is available on the website. Be sure to check it out, cast a vote to support the challenge, and join the Team Bliss Newsletter for regular updates on the progress of the challenge!

Cheat Sheets for Following Your Own Bliss

This section provides four added bonuses regarding the pursuit of happiness and how you can follow your bliss, regardless of your current circumstances. The pieces, called 'Cheat Sheets' provide tips and tricks to help anyone follow their bliss and add a little "magic" to your life to enhance the your joy. The final piece covers some tips for handling the challenges and difficulties in living this thing that we call life.

5 Tips for Identifying Your Bliss / Purpose in Life

I remember watching an interview with Anderson Cooper where he talked about the time his mom, Gloria Vanderbilt, gave him advice for life after college with the phrase "Follow Your Bliss". He rolled his eyes and recounted his reaction, which mirrored mine when I previously heard the same advice.

How do you follow your bliss if you don't know what that is? Here are five simple ways to identify your bliss.

1. What made you happy as a child, or what childhood dream have you given up?

Think about the activities you enjoyed doing when you were a carefree child (before life got in the way). Do any of these activities still appeal to you? If so, try them again, even if it is only for an hour or two.

2. What activities do you "lose yourself" in?

When you are in the "flow" time flies by, and it is a sign that you are doing something that is related to your bliss.

3. What would you do if money wasn't an issue?

As adults, we are preoccupied with paying the bills. If something doesn't look like it will be profitable, we rule it out. Following your bliss can be a hobby or part time endeavor. You don't have to pressure yourself to make your entire living from your passion, but when you are enthusiastic about what you do on any level, unexpected doors will often open to possibilities beyond your imagination.

4. What would you do if you had a day all to yourself?

Answer without thinking. The first things that pop into your head are indicators of where your bliss may be.

5. What is on your bucket list?

The higher on the bucket list an item is for you, the closer to your bliss it is likely to be. Look at what the top five items are as well as any general themes to your bucket list items. That's a clue as to where your bliss is.

While the advice to 'follow your bliss' may seem naïve, it really is a different way of addressing the nature of the purpose of your life. Honestly, the term 'purpose' and the term 'bliss' can be used interchangeably. When you are fulfilling your purpose, in whatever form that takes, you will find peace and contentment…otherwise known as bliss. It's truly a circular pattern.

5 Ways You Can Follow Your Bliss...No Matter Your Current Circumstances

Many who exist day-to-day, rather than living their dream, can have a hard time with the notion of simply flipping a proverbial switch and following their bliss. After all, by the time you reach even the earliest years of adulthood, there are realities and responsibilities to address. They grow in number and complexity as one matures as well. It sounds airy-fairy to chime "Just follow your bliss" as an answer to everything.

There is truth, however, in the statement if one of your goals in life is to feel happy and contented. The question is: "how does one balance following bliss and handling responsibility?"

1. It's not an all or nothing proposition.

Society tends to train people to think is dualities, all or nothing. If your bliss is cooking delicious meals, the traditional wisdom is that you should be a professional chef of some sort to be "successful" at following your bliss. It is typical to view ourselves and others as what they do for a living rather than where their passions lie, but there is a difference. Following your bliss and paying your way can be any combination of endeavors from a career centered around your bliss to a career that provides for your needs

111

and a part time bliss endeavor…or even just a blissful hobby. There is nothing that says your bliss must result in a paycheck. Your bliss is about your joy and your purpose. It is possible that you can turn your bliss into some sort of financial reward, but profiting is not a requirement.

2. Know what your bliss is and what it is not.

Following your bliss is a journey, not a destination. If it were a set point, the saying would say something like "Get your bliss". 'Following' implies an ongoing process that is fluid and evolving. What made you happy years ago may not be what makes you happy now or in the future. New opportunities and experiences develop constantly. You need to be open and willing to explore. It is okay to change your mind, alter your course, and seize new opportunities. Bliss is not a set point.

3. Decide what you truly want.

This is similar to the previous point and dovetails on the previous cheat sheet. You can't follow your bliss if you have no clue about what lights your fire or trips your proverbial trigger. Experimenting is fun but randomly chasing options can be exhausting and deflating as well.

To follow your bliss you have to know what it is and what you want from the experience. If you want to make your bliss your career, there are different steps you need to take to determine how to monetize it, which may or may not have anything to do with your actual performance. Are you willing to take on the extra steps to monetize your bliss? If you're not, you may need to adjust your expectations of your desired results.

Another roadblock, aside from financial hopes and fears, to following one's bliss is often the expectations of others. No one is immune from these pressures. The young, middle-aged, and seniors can all find that they listen to others more than they listen to what is inside. To truly follow your bliss, you have to listen to YOU and no one else. Others may factor in how you pursue your bliss, but your actual blissful activity is your sole privilege, opportunity, and responsibility.

4. Give yourself permission.

Here's where the "buts" make themselves known. No, I'm not talking about generous backsides. I'm talking about the excuses. All the reasons you can't, won't or don't follow your bliss will surface to keep you right where you are at. As a general rule, people tend towards what is familiar while craving the new and exciting. When taking the first steps to satisfy that craving for novelty, fear can surface in the form of excuses real and imagined, internal and external. Give yourself permission to at least try whatever it is you desire. No matter how many others present challenges, you will always be the toughest critic. Once you make up your mind, the naysayers will either go quiet or disappear altogether.

You can test the waters before making a bigger physical, financial, or time commitment. (Remember the first tidbit...it doesn't have to be all or nothing.) The simplest way to overcome the fear is to give yourself permission, verbally and in written form, to try or 'test drive' your activity. By giving yourself permission verbally, your brain hears and processes the concept as real on a deeper level. Writing and signing your own "Permission Slip" also provides validation in addition to a reminder that you are accountable to at least try. There's no excuse once you give yourself permission.

5. Own it...NOW!

Once you have given yourself permission to try and actually begin, you need to own it completely. If your bliss is running, painting, writing, building, or whatever, don't say that you are trying it. Claim the title. Instead of saying "I'm trying to run" (or paint, write, build, etc.) call yourself a runner. Once you have taken the first step, you ARE doing it. You'll find that the permitting yourself to try and then claim to "BE" lead you to follow your bliss.

5 Tips for Adding a Little Magic to Your Life

What makes me happy in my writing is celebrating "everyday magic". This usually makes people think of spells, potions, and such. Though my writing is often categorized as Magical Realism or even supernatural, everyday magic is a celebration of what makes you smile and soak up the experience that we call life. Serendipity and synchronicity are the sisters to everyday magic. Adding more of these smiling sisters to your life is simply about willingness and openness.

1. K.I.S.S.

Decide to do a "Keep-It-Simple-Sunshine" makeover to allow magic to enter your daily life. (I know the traditional phrasing of the acronym, but I don't think calling anyone 'stupid' brings about any good.) Women in particular are prone to having a weak "NO" muscle. We often agree to do too much, even when we are already booked solid. Give yourself a KISS and clear out the non-essential time suckers from your life to allow more of what you actually want and need to arrive. It will help lower your stress and raise your confidence. (After all, saying yes and struggling or not being able to follow through drains both your energy and self-esteem.) Once you strengthen your 'no' muscle in a positive way, the real opportunities have a chance to enter your life.

2. Sacred Space

You don't need a full 'man cave' or 'she shed' to have a space of your own. Space is a relative thing. Your space can be as simple as the screensaver that you have on your phone or computer or as elaborate as a room or other location. The point is to have a point of contact that provides you a breathing space when you need a reset. It may be a picture of a tropical sunset for your dream vacation. Maybe you have a little alter of sorts with some of your favorite things. Alters don't have to be religious or challenge any of your spiritual practices. Again, it is a place where you can focus and hit the reset button whenever necessary. When you are refreshed, you can see opportunity and feel joy more readily.

3. Ask for and Look for Signs

I have found that when I feel lost, I am totally disconnected down to the emotional and spiritual level. Even though I know that I am never completely alone, it can feel like I am when life appears to be overwhelming. I may not see all of my options because of a natural "fight or flight" reaction to circumstances. Before I get to the point of that panic or despair, I ask for a sign. Sometimes the request is simply to reassure myself that I am indeed not alone. Other times, a sign is for a course of action. Signs can take all types of forms. It could be a repeated and meaningful number seen multiple times. Maybe it's a word or phrase that is surprisingly "right on time". It could be an actual object in the form of a feather, coin, or picture that arrives. It may not be coincidence when that special song plays on the radio or the person that has just the right advice calls you out of the blue. I have had all of these experiences at one point or another. To keep the channels to this type of

116

magic/assistance open, all that is necessary is to be willing to ask, be open to what happens, and be grateful for the assistance that does arrive.

4. Dream and Give Yourself a Kiss

This exercise was given to me by a Reiki practitioner after I confided that I felt stuck in my life and missed experiencing joy. It's best done in a little unlined notebook to keep a trail of your daily progress.

The Set Up:

- First, make a small box in the middle of the page and put the date inside of it.
- Draw a diagonal line out from the top left corner. At the end of that line, write the word "DREAM" and circle it, leaving enough room to write words or phrases.
- Draw a similar line out from the top right corner, and label the circle or bubble "TO DO"
- Repeat with the bottom right with the label "FEELINGS"
- Finish the set up in the bottom left with a doodle of a piece of candy (the practitioner suggested a Hershey's Kiss as a symbol of a little sweat treat). If you don't want to doodle then write "TREAT"

The Exercise:

- Return to the "DREAM" area and brainstorm 1-3 things you can do TODAY to pursue your dream. Make them true action steps, but they need to be possible to complete in the next 24 hours. Don't fret if you don't have a dream to work towards. Identifying a dream may be your task for the day. It is important to keep it manageable. For example, if your dream is to move across the country, you probably won't complete that dream in 24 hours. Instead, make your dream tasks something like: research housing options/neighborhoods, find out moving costs, or set a date.

- At the "TO DO" area list 3-5 things that MUST be done in the next 24 hours. Do not overwhelm yourself with these tasks. What needs to be done today to live peacefully? Do you have a certain meeting that you must attend? List it. Is there a bill that must be paid? Add it. Do you have an appointment with a dentist, doctor, or mechanic? Put it down. Is there shopping to be done? You get the idea. You're not curing cancer, hunger, or the status of world peace here. You are simply taking care of business.

- At the "FEELINGS" section free write how you are feeling at the very moment. Include all feelings, good, bad, and indifferent. The point is to simply acknowledge and get them all out. Unburden yourself or celebrate your happiness. This is just for you...no one will judge.

- Now, at the kiss or "TREAT" section, have some fun. Think of 3 things that you can do for yourself today as a reward. These are little bonuses, just for you. Maybe it is literally a piece of chocolate. It could be walking around the block to get some fresh air or even walking barefoot on the grass in the yard. You could decide to read a book for 20 minutes before sleeping or possibly soaking in the tub. A mug of special tea or coffee may do the trick too. The point is to make part of your daily routine an intentional reward for living life. You don't have to be superhuman to deserve a reward for getting through your day. In essence, you start your day by focusing on your dreams and work through it all to end with a reward.

You'll be surprised how the weight of your day begins to feel more manageable and opportunities to celebrate actually lighten your load.

5. Give A Little, Receive A Lot

A little secret that philanthropists understand is that helping others actually creates a circular effect that comes back bigger and stronger than the effort you expend. Yes, we are all incredibly busy (especially if you overlooked the first tidbit), but giving doesn't have to be grandiose. You don't have to organize a fundraising gala or join the board of a charitable organization. It can be as simple as helping an elderly person get their groceries in the car at the store or taking their cart back for them. Maybe you pay it forward for the next person in line and treat them to a surprise. You can reach out with a card or email to someone with whom you've lost contact. Even letting a mother jump ahead with her squirming child in the bathroom line can provide an unexpected boost.

At some point, you'll start noticing that these little things come back your way in all types of serendipitous encounters that provide a little bit of magic to your day.

I have faced many challenges from caring for disabled and terminally ill family members to death, job loss, and lost opportunities of all types. You may not be able to see it in the moment, but everything that happens in life is a blessing or a lesson. Sometimes it's a combination of both. The real difference between diving or surviving is in how you chose to view a situation. I like to think that challenges are a dare to rise to a better circumstance rather than a roadblock to happiness.

119

Tips for Handling Loss, Change & Challenges

I am not a therapist, but I know quite a bit about dealing with loss and life's curveballs. While writing *Triangulating Bliss*, I dealt with my dad's terminal cancer diagnosis and his passing. Months later, my sister passed away from complications related to her life-long disability. This was all at the same time I was dealing with rapid changes in my career field, my job ending, and other life challenges. It was tough, to say the least.

I don't have all the answer, but I do have 5 tips for surviving the "dark night of the soul" and hanging tough until the sunrises once again.

1. Think ahead.

You don't have to become a Doomsday Prepper, but a little forethought makes a dark moment a bit easier. I know from experience, when my dad died New Year's night I was faced with finding a mortuary in the predawn hours (on the day after a major holiday) when the staff insisted that we have everything in order before the family returned home. I knew dad's general wishes, but there were no specifics. It led to a long journey which was costly both emotionally and financially. Having a bit of a game plan before disaster makes a difficult situation less traumatic.

2. Give yourself time.

In line with the previous tip, don't be afraid to insist on the time necessary to process your circumstances before committing to anything. Regardless of whether you have suffered the loss of a loved one, a job, a relationship or another opportunity, you don't have to react in a "shoot from the hip" manner. There are different degrees of loss, and everyone handles situations differently. It can take up to a year for the dust to settle after a major life crisis. A little time is not an unreasonable request, no matter what anyone else says.

3. Beware of "sneaker moments".

Everyone grieves differently. There are different time frames and varying methods for coping with loss. It doesn't matter whether the loss is major or minor. There will be times that anger or sadness may pop up, and it is often unexpected. Give yourself a couple of minutes to feel the sadness, grief, or anger, and then make it a point to look for the good in the experience. It will help you reset more quickly than staying frozen in the hurt.

4. Honor the loss.

Whether you have lost someone or something through death or a simple change of circumstance, recognizing and honoring what was is an easy way to begin the healing process. Honoring the loss can be as simple as writing a letter stating how you feel followed by what you learned from the experience (even if you never mail it). A personal and meaningful ritual can also work. It could be serving a lost loved one's favorite food, engaging in an event that is meaningful, burning a candle in honor, watching a sunrise or sunset, or anything else that feels right.

5. There's no shame in calling in reinforcements.

Don't be afraid to ask for help. Most people are happy to assist if asked, but they won't volunteer unless they know there is a need. You don't have to do everything by yourself. If you find that you are still having problems dealing with daily living months after a loss, don't be afraid to seek professional guidance. There are a number of support groups for any number of situations, and mental health resources are available, even for those with financial considerations.

Extended Excerpt of *Triangulating Self*

Teaser

Phil Atwater is the beloved owner of a neighborhood hangout called *Our Place*. One moment he is alive and preparing for a New Year's Eve party. The next he is approached by someone who he's never seen and confirms that his reality is changed forever.

Now Phil confronts the nature of human existence:

- What happens after you die?
- Do good people automatically go to Heaven?
- Is there really a Heaven and a Hell?
- What happens if you have unfinished business when you draw your last breath?

Phil's sudden death opens a door between the world - as he once knew it - and what lies beyond. To find his eternal bliss, he must make peace with his earthly past. Not only does Phil's eternity depend on it, but also the lives of seven other people are subject on his success. As Phil embarks on a quest to complete his unfinished business, it raises more questions for the seven, seemingly random, people who experience Phil's handiwork in the *Bliss Triangle*.

Can Phil and the 'Seven' figure out what it takes to find peace and ensure a bliss-filled future? It all begins by walking through the right door, at the right time. Find out about the origins of the mysterious Bliss Triangle in *Triangulating Self.*

Thanks to the nature of the universe and of time itself, it's not quite a prequel or even a sequel. Let's just call it a tandem to *Triangulating Bliss.*

Excerpt

Note: This is still a work in progress which is due for future release...consider it a true behind-the-scenes, sneak peek of what is in the works.

December 31, 2009: 7:59 p.m. (Pacific Time)
Now (Universal Time)
Day 1 (Transition Time)

It happened that quickly. The blink of an eye, a heartbeat, a New York minute all had nothing on this. I was sitting in bed watching the most beautiful woman in the world, my wife, scavenging through her closet for a dress to wear. We had a New Year's Eve party to get to, and we'd just finished loving each other like eager teenagers, rather than card carrying members of the senior discount crowd. My heart swelled with love, and I felt so blessed. I wanted to laugh from the joy. Instead, a white light hit. It wasn't lighting, but my time was up that quick.

There was no whoosh. I didn't float out of my body. One moment I was in my body, and the next I was standing on the other side of the room watching the heartbreak unfold.

"How about this one?" Lois spun around in front of the closet, holding up a colorful dress.

Her smile dropped immediately when she saw me. "Phil! What's wrong?" She leapt towards the bed and caught my body as my head dropped to the mattress.

"I love you!" I screamed from where I was now, but this mouth didn't move. Instead, my body on the bed gasped, "Love…" Then I felt everything flowing back into what I am now. I'm not sure what that is at this point, but I'm more concerned about Lois. Heaviness hit as my wife of thirty years let out a soul crushing wail.

Instantly, I was back by her side. I could feel her pain as if it was my own. "Make it stop!" I shouted again without actually speaking.

"Phil!" A soothing yet authoritative voice boomed.

I looked to the spot I where I had been watching the scene unfold and saw a luminescent being. It wasn't a ghost. It was a bit more solid than that. It wasn't an angel in the way you'd expect. You know, there weren't any wings or heavenly music. I couldn't make out if it was a man or a woman either. I was greeted with a knowing smile as the being seemed to understand that I was trying to make sense of it all.

"Yes, Phil, you have left that body," the being explained without any mouth movement, yet I heard it clearly.

"I want to go back. I have to be with her. I have to make it okay."

"What's done is done," the being explained. "It is time to transition."

"No, I need to stay."

"That's not possible. Phil, your time is done. It's time to transition."

I looked at Lois and the crumpled body that was so familiar from seven decades of inhabiting it. Lois pulled my body to the floor and began CPR. As she moved from rescue breaths to compressions, she muttered, "Come on, Phil. Come on." Tears streamed down her face.

"I have to help her. She's all alone."

The being smiled at me as if there was a secret.

The phone rang next to the bed. Lois ignored it and began to scream out. "NO! Phil please don't leave me!" Lois gasped for breath as her face contorted. "I love you so much," she added in barely more than a whisper.

I could feel her emotion, love and anguish combined. "Come on honey. Accept the help. Let someone know that you need help." I willed to her.

The phone rang again. The happy ringtone was such a jarring contrast to the pained scene. Again, Lois made no move to pick it up. I wanted to pick it up and at least get someone to hear her distress, but I couldn't.

"Lois!" A woman's voice filled the room. Jean, our friend and neighbor, ran to Lois's side. "Are you okay? What happened?" Before Lois could answer, Jean studied my body and shouted, "Oh God."

"H-h-h-he c-c-c-col-l-lapsed," Lois choked as she transitioned back to compressions.

"Keep working. I'm calling 911." Jean had the phone to her ear.

Once the ambulance arrived and the body - my body - was taken, I turned my attention to my companion. "Who are you?"

"You can call me Jeremiel. I'm here to help you with your transition."

"Why now?"

Jeremiel chuckled. "That's the most common question that I get from new returns. The answer is simple...It was time."

I felt the weight from Lois's heartbreak once more as I watched Jean attempt to give her some tea while she sat in a daze on the couch. She looked so lost and fragile despite how strong I knew her to be. I didn't care about myself or my new reality. I just wanted to ease her pain. I went to her side and put my hand to her cheek. It was as if she could feel me. Her hand came up to the same spot on her face. All I could do was send love and hope that she could feel it.

129

"She does," Jeremiel interrupted.

I turned. "There's really no going back now, is there?"

"Every spirit has free will, but there are complications if you don't embrace what is. I can't stop you from staying, but I suggest you come and learn about this reality before you make a decision," Jeremiel reached out. "You can return in your present form as you need and want, but there are some things to know before you lock yourself in-between."

I sighed and studied the love of my life. I saw Lois as I'd always seen her. Beautiful. Her hair dark, her feisty yet compassionate personality, her heart…the biggest I ever had the pleasure of sharing. She taught me that real love was possible, and her reward was to have to deal with this all by herself. There was a burning deep inside me. I wanted to protect her and make this right for her.

"Lesson one," Jeremiel began. "Time is far more fluid than you think. Come with me. Learn about your options. She's not alone. She may feel like she is, but people are never without the assistance they need. It's possible to be here at a moment's notice if you want to be."

"I'll never leave you, love," I murmured as placed a kiss atop Lois's head. I took a deep breath and turned to Jeremiel. "Let's do this then."

080

Just as quickly as I left my body, I was in the most beautiful meadow with the bluest skies. Tall waving grasses surrounded me as I looked out over a crystal clear stream. Jeremiel was again by my side. The feeling of peace and well-being was all-encompassing.

"How do you feel?" Jeremiel broke into my thoughts.

"Amazing," I replied. Even that word didn't describe it, and I began to hum.

Jeremiel smiled. "That's a good sign."

"So, this is heaven?"

"Heaven is a physical being concept. We don't use it here. What you're thinking of is better described as 'The All' or 'The Everything' which is still a plane or two from here. This is more of a transition zone."

"Okay. Is this where I do my life review?"

Jeremiel made a musical sound that I assumed was a laugh. "Again, that's something the physicals like to perpetuate. There's no guilt trip here, so you don't go back and rehash the imperfections of human existence. Every human is imperfect. That's just the nature of the life course. Instead, there's a process to make sure your spirit is at peace with the experience of a life journey."

"I get it...No Book of Life." I still wasn't clear though. "How does this other process work?"

Jeremiel bent over near the edge of the water and picked up a brilliant clear crystal. "Right, there's no book, but this crystal holds all of the answers."

He held it up as I watched the light dance from it.

"It holds your accomplishments, your agreements made both in life and before birth, as well as your challenges."

"Challenges?"

"Like I said, there's no guilt here, but new returns often have ties or unfinished business that they need to resolve in order to find complete peace. You can't enter into the All until you have total peace."

I smiled. "I feel pretty amazing now. In fact, I don't think I have ever felt better, so that shouldn't be a problem."

Jeremiel returned the smile. "This is only a fraction of all that is possible. The fact that you have embraced the feeling thus far is a good sign. You are ready for the next step."

"And that is?"

"Let's take a walk," Jeremiel motioned.

I followed, though it was more of a floating transport, to a large mirror trimmed in gold.

I beamed at my reflection. Instead of the senior citizen who collapsed on the bed, I looked like I did in my forties. My eyes shined bright blue. My hair was full and dark. I had a glow similar to Jeremiel's. "I look good!" I flexed my muscles.

Then I noticed my hand. No longer mangled and missing pieces, my left hand was once again complete. I laughed and moved it. All the fingers and the thumb were present and alternated between opened and closed at my command. "I haven't had that hand since Korea!"

"Even in the transition zone, the All makes everyone whole," Jeremiel watched me flex my hand. "What do you see?"

"I see a younger me," I answered.

"Yes, you still have some things to learn and consider before your transition is complete."

I held up the crystal. "This told you that?"

"No, the fact that you are still attached to your physical body tells me that. When your transition is complete, you will be pure light and energy."

I studied Jeremiel. "So, you're not complete. I mean your body looks a lot like mine."

"When we assist in the transition process, especially when we do retrievals, we take a form that matches the spirit that we are helping. You'll see what I mean."

Jeremiel motioned to the mirror and tapped it. The surface rippled like water. "You are ready for the next step. My work at this stage is done. If you would like more of my help, you just have to call me. You'll be meeting your transition coach through there. That's where you'll get all the information that you need to make your decision about how to go forward."

I must have looked as confused as I felt.

"You've proven you're ready. It's time to take the next step, but you need to do it on your own."

I began to move towards the surface.

"It's been a pleasure," Jeremiel's voice followed me through the portal.

A large light-filled room greeted me on the other side of the mirror. Music surrounded me. The place was crowded with a variety of people. Some looked like me. Some were a bit more solid. Then there were other masses of light circulating.

A pleasantly glowing being joined me immediately, "Hello. Welcome. Do you have your crystal?"

I held it up. "Yes."

The being looked at the crystal. "Ah...okay. Camael will be your Transition Coach. There will be a quick reception, and then you will have your personalized consultation. Please feel free to relax. Would you like some elixir while you wait?"

"Elixir?"

"It's kind of a drink."

"Like wine? I didn't think eating and drinking happened after death."

"It's hard to explain to a new return. You'll learn about that with Camael. Think of it as anything you want it to be...energy, drink, food, whatever. I highly recommend it."

"Sure. Why not?"

The goblet appeared in my hand immediately. It was a golden color. "Bottoms up," I cheered towards the room in general. The delicious concoction was a cross between my favorite soda pop, wine, and the bourbon that I loved to partake of on special occasions. I sighed and began to wander around the ballroom.

The more solid looking folk seemed to congregate along the edges of the room. Many were seated. They appeared the most confused and distressed. I smiled when one made eye contact, but she looked away quickly. The smoky crystal resting on her lap glinted in the light.

Those that looked like me were strolling throughout the room. They seemed more relaxed and willing to make eye contact. All carried bright and shiny crystals like mine. It reminded me of being at the airport. The ones on the sides were like those who weren't happy to return home from a vacation, while the lighter ones were excited to head off on an adventure.

Then there were the ones that were simply bundles of light. There were orbs and streaks and morphing shapes in constant motion. I couldn't help but smile and laugh as I watched them. It was like watching a pack of energetic puppies playing and enjoying life. It was quite a show. There didn't appear to be a reason to worry as long as I didn't focus on the people along the edges of the room who were weighed down.

My attention shifted upward from the light beings. The ceiling gave way to a brilliant light, and the playful light beings began to float towards the opening as it became too blinding to watch any further. I shifted my gaze to the glistening silvery floor that looked like the mirror portal that brought me into the ballroom.

When the light dimmed, the playful souls were all gone. The people along the edges looked even more uncomfortable while those like me wore amused expressions.

"Now it is time for those of you with the darkened crystals to come this way," a deep baritone voice boomed. I couldn't see who it came from, but the solid people complied. They made their way to a curtain at the back of the room and exited in silence.

Immediately following the last person's exit behind the curtain, a shining being appeared beside me cloaked in a golden yellow light that reminded me of saffron. The face looked vaguely recognizable in the glow.

"Hello Phil. My name is Camael. I was one of your guardian angels at birth." Just like Jeremiel, Camael's mouth didn't move, but I heard every word.

"Is that why you seem familiar?"

"Most likely. I wasn't your only guardian, but I was there from the start. You had several over the course of your life journey."

"Do you need this?" I raised my crystal.

134

"No. I know everything about you already. That's more for you. Would you like to start your consultation?"

"Yes."

We were transported to a comforting spot. Camael and I were at the end of the dock at the lake, in front of the inn I once owned. Many of the moments in my life when I sought comfort or refuge, I ended up in that very spot.

"How are you?"

"Personally, I am great. I've never felt better, even if I don't understand everything yet. I do have some concerns about my wife though."

"It's good that you are embracing the peace even with some heaviness for who is left behind. It's a good sign. I'm here to help you understand and decide how to move forward."

I laughed. "When I got to the ballroom, they said that you were my transition coach."

"That's a good way to think about the process. Let's start with your most pressing questions." Camael appeared to bob as if to encourage me to speak. "Go for it."

"I really want to ask why, but it seems irrelevant at this point."

Camael chuckled. "Yeah, that's to be expected, especially given the circumstances of your return."

"Meaning?"

"You went quickly, without any real warning signs that you could identify in advance. It can make the return a bit more challenging because of unfinished business."

"So, what exactly took me out anyway?"

"Brain aneurysm. You once asked that it be quick when it happened." Camael made a throaty sound. "Double edged sword on that one."

"Mmmm." *What can I say to that one?* I thought as I watched the sunlight dance on the water for some time. There was the smallest part of me that still wanted to fight against the unavoidable nature of my circumstances.

"Are you ready to learn more about the process, or would you like me to leave you to yourself for a while longer?"

I felt like I had to keep moving on. Stalling wasn't an option even with the twinge of unease. "I'm okay. It's time to deal with it."

"Let's begin with an overview."

I nodded in agreement.

"You are currently in transition. Some spirits are ready to go directly to the All. Others are set to return immediately to address more learning and lessons. Then there is another group of spirits who are on the verge of being ready to go to the next plane, but they are held back for one or more reasons. You, Phil, are one of those souls that sit on the verge."

I rubbed my hands together, still marveling at my returned hand. "What did I do wrong? What do I have to do to move on?"

"It's not that you necessarily did anything wrong. We don't work with dualities like right and wrong. You're in pretty good shape. You lived a good life. The fact is that you have some unresolved business that you haven't released yet. Those are easy enough to remedy. The real challenge might surprise you though."

Scenes from my life flashed in my mind. Growing up without a mom. Feeling like dad blamed me for her death. The nightmare on the lines in Korea. Losing Allison and the baby. The years that followed. The vision of Lois screaming out at the moment the aneurysm burst.

"Nope," Cameal interrupted. "None of those, though they are a part of the resolution process. Your biggest challenge isn't regret for something you think was bad. Your biggest challenge is the fact that you found true and unconditional love with Lois."

I sat back in shock. "Loving Lois is my biggest problem," *How can love keep me from heaven…or whatever it's considered here?* "That makes no sense."

136

"Love is indeed the most powerful thing across all planes of reality. It is truly what existence is all about." Camael motioned for Phil to follow.

Together, they journeyed along the shoreline and watched a family. The mother and father joked with each other while keeping an eye on their son and daughter romping in the shallow cove. They played ball with a bouncing, black and white border collie.

"What do you think that mother would do for her children?" Camael asked.

"Most likely, anything she can."

"How about the father? What would he do for his family?"

I studied the man. I had a deep knowing that he would give his all for any of them to be happy. "The same. Anything."

"Would he lay down his life to make sure that his wife was protected?"

The way the man looked at the woman was apparent. "Yes."

"He has the same look in his eyes that you always had with Lois."

I smiled as I saw myself in him now. "She was the best thing that ever happened to me."

"You were blessed to have found that. Many miss the opportunity because they don't allow it in." Camael observed.

"It wasn't an easy road to get there."

"I know. I was with you the whole time, even in those darkest of days."

I laughed though the thought of those years wasn't pleasant.

"Here's the deal," Camael began. "You are still deeply tied to each other. You both have to make peace with things as they are now in order for you to move forward. Do you remember the vow you took before you left Lois?"

"What vow?"

"You said that you'd never leave her," Camael explained.

It flashed in my mind. That was my parting comment to Lois before following Jeremiel.

"That vow created a problem for your transition. She heard you…in her heart. Until you decide how you are going to handle that vow, you will be stuck in transition."

"Okay. I'll just wait for her here." *That's easy enough. I spent 30 years waiting for her. I can wait some more.*

Camael shook his head. "It's not quite that simple."

I felt a tightness course through my body. It felt like forever before Camael explained.

"There's a 90-day transition window for new returns. Granted, time works differently on this plane of reality. It's not 90 days like it was on Earth. Time is more fluid for you now. In universal time there is no past or future, just the now."

"Okay. So how can there be a 90-day rule when there is just the now?"

Camael appeared to hiccup or maybe it was an uncomfortable chuckle. "The truth of the matter is that you aren't fully transitioned, so universal time doesn't fully apply to you yet. You're in-between and still subjected to elements of both time patterns. Hence, you have 90 days to make a decision about your transition."

I couldn't get my brain to grasp the nature of my predicament. "What exactly do I have to decide?"

"You have 90 days to decide whether to complete the transition process by resolving your challenges. If you don't complete the process, you can choose to return to life's classroom…"

I interrupted. "So…"

Camael's head shook as halted my question. "In that case, you'll return as a new and different person to take a chance on the nature of your next life course. The alternative is that you become a wayward spirit."

"Wayward…I already feel that way," I muttered.

"You're far from it. A wayward spirit is some who didn't complete the transition but refused to return for a new life course. You remain as the being you are now, but you can't go to the All on your own. You also can't return to your previous life. In essence you are stuck, possibly forever, in-between. It's not the worst thing to happen, but you give up the best of what is available to you."

"The choice is save myself and leave Lois forever or stay in limbo indefinitely," I wanted to yell at the Universe. "What you're saying is give up on my love or give up on myself?"

"It's not quite that bleak," Camael tried to calm me. "As I said, all of existence is reliant on love, but ultimately you have to understand yourself to complete the transition."

There was a weight in my body at the thought of leaving Lois behind forever. It felt like a huge cord was pulling at my heart. I looked down and that's exactly what it looked like. A thick cord of light was coming out of my chest.

"As much as you feel that way about Lois, she feels that way about you. It's beautiful to see that love between two people, but that's also the problem. If each of you can't make peace with the situation, you both will be stuck in a half existence. You have to do your part. She has to do hers. That's the reason that I have been assigned to coach you."

"It sounds daunting."

"It can be. You saw the ones carrying the darkened crystals at the reception, right?"

"Yes."

"They are the ones who faced the decision regarding wayward status. It's a far bigger and important decision to make than simply returning for another life course. It could mean an existence of less than for the rest of eternity."

"This is all a bit much." I sighed. *Maybe a life review and gate keeper at heaven's door would have been easier.*

139

"Listen, there is a lot of work to do, but there is time as well. It's quite a bit to take in a single conversation, and we've barely scratched the surface. I hit you with the biggest challenge that you face. I figured it was better that way. If you get that one, everything falls into place fairly easily."

I half asked, half stated, "I have to decide to never see Lois again."

Camael stopped. "No. While you are in transition, you have the ability to visit. Yes, it's in spirit form rather than physical, but you can go back and forth and take care of business."

I knew what I had to do. "In that case," I began. "I need to go to Lois. Now."

To get additional sneak peeks of *Triangulating Self*, as well as special opportunities, join the "Team Bliss" Newsletter for more tips and tricks for following your bliss as well as Janelle's upcoming releases and appearances.

Sign up now at TriangulatingBliss.com.

The Mystique of Living Series

It wasn't until late in the process that the idea of creating a series from my "Bliss Baby" emerged. Phil's story was the first to scream out to be told, but his tale wasn't the only one. Stay tuned, not only for Triangulating Self, but also the other stories that make up the *Mystique of Living Series.* Sure, it may have been obvious to go with "The Triangulating Series", but at the core of the Bliss journey, the message is simple. We are all working to understand this sometimes surreal thing called life. That process may be done by triangulating things as Henri claims, but really it's about engaging in the mystique of life. When defined 'Mystique' means 'a fascinating aura of mystery, awe, and power surrounding someone or something.' That 'something' in this case is life itself. I hope you enjoy the ride as the series develops.

Triangulating Self (Phil's Story) – Coming 2016

Triangulating Wisdom – Coming 2016

    Part 1: Mikel's Story

    Part 2: Dee's Story

Triangulating Love (Sara & Henri's Story) – TBA

Triangulating Abundance (Richard's Story) – TBA

About the Author

Janelle Jalbert discovered her passions at the age of 10. One was teaching as she taught stuffed animals daily lessons. The other was writing, due to her love of reading. After reading about an aspiring writer in her favorite book series, the light bulb clicked on, and Jalbert said "I want to do that!" Thus, her writing career began with serialized stories for her friends in the form notes passed before class.

Then, the cries to pursue a "stable" career beat her dreams of writing.

After college, Jalbert taught language arts and writing at all levels. While in the classroom, students teased Jalbert for her love of auto racing. Her reply was simply "Smart girls love racing too". While deciding on a topic for her master's thesis, Jalbert stumbled into the world of Magical Realism and was hooked, though at first it was limited to an academic interest. Jalbert wrote while teaching including an educational book, contributing to a business book, blogging and reporting on education. Once Jalbert transitioned to online teaching, she simultaneously taught and served as a motorsports reporter while traveling the country for racing events.

Jalbert had an epiphany in the fall of 2013. Listening to a nagging voice inside, Jalbert began a story that would shape a new path in her life. The voice stated that she had 30 days to get the novel written. It sounded illogical and melodramatic, but she began drafting. It was nearly 30 days later when her father was diagnosed with a brain tumor, followed by other advanced cancers. It was during the remaining weeks with her dad that Jalbert completed the initial draft of *Triangulating Bliss,* though it would take two years for the novel to be published.

In the months following her father's death, Jalbert's professional focus became writing and pursuing her dream. She began copywriting, landing projects from individual professionals to leading businesses. Copywriting led to numerous ghostwriting opportunities from international clients. With that momentum, Jalbert pitched and landed the contract for a book titled *Wine for Beginners.*

Throughout the spring and summer of 2014, Jalbert juggled copywriting, ghostwriting, fiction writing, and writing the wine book. On the morning that she submitted the draft of *Wine for Beginners* to the publisher, Jalbert went to celebrate with her mother and sister, only to find that life had other plans. Less than 12 hours later, Jalbert's sister lost her 14 year battle with health complications related to a life-long disability.

Jalbert's belief in the magic of daily life was both shattered and later reaffirmed as a result of her life-changing year. It is that belief, and the desire to help others see a special side to this crazy thing called life, that fuels her writing.

In addition to teaching and writing, Jalbert loves to explore the world. Jalbert has traveled throughout Japan, Australia, Europe, the United States and other destinations. Her travels are often solo ventures with as little as a wallet, backpack and passport. In addition to auto racing, her guilty pleasures include happily-ever-after stories in book or film form, a glass or two of good wine, and cooking therapy. Jalbert currently lives in Southern California with her rescue pups and regularly returns to her second home in North Carolina. To learn more about her current and upcoming releases and promotions visit www.janellejalbert.com.

5 Fun Facts You Didn't Know About Me:

- I was valedictorian of my preschool class. When I stood to speak at graduation, I had no clue about what to say. I panicked, and blurted "I LOVE YOU!" before sitting back down.
- My love of travel started at age 8 with a 5 week car **trip around the country. It was dad, mom, grandma,** sister and me, stuffed in a small station wagon back in the days that kids could still play in the back without car seats.
- When I graduated from middle school, everyone thought I was going to be a seismologist or geologist because my science fair project on earthquakes took top honors and went all the way to the state science fair. I have always had a weakness for collecting rocks.
- My number one comfort food is chili cheese fries. It started with a high school friend who introduced me to a local burger shack that had chili cheese fries and pineapple milkshakes. (I know...what a combo!)
- I often joke that I should have been a truck driver, especially when my student loans are due. I love driving and have been known to take off with little notice and drive all over the country. My favorite time behind the wheel is sunrise while going eastbound on a long-haul road trip. (I think that goes back to fun fact #2.)

Connect

Janelle welcomes readers to connect with her as well as with the Team Bliss effort.

Websites:

www.janellejalbert.com
www.triangulatingbliss.com

Sign Up for the Team Bliss Newsletter:
www.triangulatingbliss.com/Newsletter

Connect on Social Media:
Twitter
www.twitter.com/justjjwriting
www.twitter.com/TriBliss

Facebook
www.facebook.com/janellejalbert.author

Goodreads Author Page
http://www.goodreads.com/Janelle_Jalbert

www.ingramcontent.com/pod-product-compliance
Lightning Source LLC
Chambersburg PA
CBHW050952120626
46552CB00001B/495